Deeper Six

Julie Bergman

Deeper Six

Julie Bergman

Undercover Books

Published in the United States by Undercover Books
Library of Congress Control
Number: 2023924049

ISBN (paperback) 979-8-9856037-5-0
ISBN (hardback) 979-8-9856037-6-7
ISBN (e-book) 979-8-9856037-7-4

Extracts of verse from *Los Angeles Fires of the Heart* and *The Finder, Poems of
a Private Investigator* by Julie Bergman are used with permission.

Book design: Isaac Hernández de Lipa

Manufactured in the United States of America
First Printing 2024 Los Angeles, California

*For my friends George and Florence Lowden,
and Irene and Alan Aston, along with the
members of the Royal North of Ireland Yacht
Club, who opened my eyes and heart to the
beauty of Northern Ireland and its people*

ACKNOWLEDGMENTS

I would like to acknowledge some of the many friends who offered encouragement regarding my fiction writing, including Lee Casey, Walker Berwick, Sue Pelino, Sue Ennis, Ursula Delaroch-Vernet Stroetzel, Nancy Wilson, James White, Sheila McElwee, and Kate Cooper. Thank you to Therese Kosterman and Elena Devivo for reviewing preliminary drafts of this work.

I would also like to thank Los Angeles County Firefighter Specialist Steve Frilot and Captain John Driscoll for answering my questions about boat fires, and Chief of Police Jeremiah J. Hart, of the Torrance, California Police Department, and former San Diego Police Detective Kathleen Mauzy for providing an overview of city versus federal involvement regarding offshore crimes. Lastly, thank you to Dr. Ridge Muller for guidance regarding the depiction of medical emergencies.

CHAPTER ONE

Whatever was lost, I was assigned
to find it.
It didn't matter that I was ten.
That was always my job.

An armed stand-off was occurring at the Will Rogers State Beach as I was driving home on Pacific Coast Highway. The moon was rising over the Pacific Palisades cliffs on the opposite side of the road as I approached Temescal Canyon Boulevard. Juxtaposed with the cosmic harmony occurring overhead, one lonely and agitated sheriff was directing cars to keep moving, trying to get the cars that had slowed on both sides of the street out of harm's way. Law enforcement vehicles were circling like a wagon train in the beach parking lot and disgorging a platoon of officers in full swat gear.

Shots were fired as I passed directly parallel to the melee on the beach. There was no telling which direction the weapon was pointed or who pulled the trigger. I pushed the button labeled 'sport' on the BMW console and jammed my foot down on the gas at the urgent behest of the traffic cop. My driving machine lurched through the red light at the intersection of Temescal Canyon and PCH. I found myself hoping there would be no bullet holes in my passenger side door, the impact of which I might not have heard against the burst of my car's powertrain. Vehicle puncture wounds would be costly. German built cars are so expensive to fix.

I continued to drive south along the western edge of the continent with the windows open, attempting to shake off the cortisol burst pounding in my heart after avoiding the live fire. Sirens wailed behind me. I pulled over and resisted the impulse to duck. Seconds later, a souped-up Chevy passed me going way over the 45 MPH speed limit, followed by several patrol cars in full pursuit.

It was just another day in Los Angeles. Nothing about this town surprised me anymore. When I moved here from Boston twenty years ago things were quieter, but this was my LA now. Crime was increasing, homelessness was rampant, traffic was often unbearable, the air was full of unhealthy particles, and too often, I ran into the wrong kinds of people in my day job.

Marina del Rey, where I lived on a 45-foot Tiara Sovern cabin cruiser tucked in off Santa Monica Bay, still provided some peace, despite the growing chaos of Los Angeles County. I pulled into the parking structure and after I turned off the engine and got out of the car, I walked around it to make sure there were no holes. There were none.

I walked down the ramp toward my boat and thanked my lucky stars that I did not get stuck in the chaos, because I had a plane to catch to meet a client in Northern Ireland - an 8:00 PM red-eye flight to London, followed by a short flight to Belfast. I'd been sent a plane ticket to meet with an Irishman about a missing family member he was hoping against hope I could find. His daughter was likely dead, but even if I could shed some daylight on the circumstances of her passing for her family's sake, the mission would be worthwhile.

My private investigative firm, which consisted of myself and a few colleagues who pitched in as needed, had developed a reputation for finding those who were missing, whether they knew or not that someone wanted to find them, or in cases where they were irretrievably lost, discovering the circumstances. In between cases, I wrote some poetry, walked a lot, and sometimes took care of other people's dogs or cats, since I traveled too often to have my own.

I was born in Massachusetts within the mixed confines of an Irish and Scottish family tree, but I migrated to LA in my twenties. I love the Pacific Coast and especially the year-round boating season, but while I find myself inexorably drawn back to my hometown of Boston, it's the islands much further east that have the greatest pull. The green isles of the UK and Ireland are magnetic home ports, and when I am lucky enough to have clients there needing my assistance, I am on a plane without hesitation.

CHAPTER TWO

"This is where she was found," Daniel Collins said, pointing to the shallows along the edge of the channel just after we'd met up outside Waterfront Hall on the way to my hotel in Northern Ireland. "Nora's body washed up here. The coroner said she'd been in the water a couple of days from the looks of her."

"How did she die?" I asked, gently.

"It was ruled a suicide, and definitely was that. There was CCTV footage of her going in of her own volition at the Albert Bridge. She'd been very despondent, and had drugs in her system, so even if she'd survived the fall, she wouldn't have been well equipped to survive."

He fought back tears as he spoke. The pain surrounded and smothered him. I could see it in his face and the slope of his shoulders, even in the low light of a wet March evening along the River Lagan in Belfast. It wasn't his only loss, and not even the one I was there to discuss.

"Let's go inside and talk," I said, motioning to the lighted ramp of a retired vessel that was now a restaurant on the quiet river that led to the former Titanic berth and further along to the Belfast docks and the Irish Sea.

We walked up the wet ramp to Holohan's at the Barge, into the small foyer and turned left, entering a warm pub scene where food and drink were being dished out to locals, the tourist season not yet in swing.

We took seats at the small bar near the end of the barge's main cabin and ordered pints from an attentive crew member. I started taking the measure of Daniel Collins, whom I'd just met after the flight to Belfast City Airport following the change of planes at Heathrow. He had lost his youngest daughter for certain in the waters of the River Lagan, but it was his oldest daughter, who disappeared a few months after her sister's suicide, who had not yet been found.

"You come highly recommended by the pride of Edinburgh," Daniel said, putting down his glass and wiping off some drops of ale that had spilled onto the sleeve of his well-worn Barbour. The fifty-something Irishman, about my height at 5'5" with damp, curly black hair, and a couple days growth of beard, smiled at me politely, as though he'd maintained enough of his inner spirit to ponder an inside joke. I have no idea what my dear Scottish friend might have told him of our relationship.

"Aiden Lindsay will be getting a big head if he hears you referring to him as that. He's one of dozens of best-selling fiction authors in Scotland. Edinburgh breeds them. How do you know each other?" I asked.

"I was at university with Aiden. I was raised in Dublin, got a degree in Edinburgh, then moved back to Dublin to work for an investment firm after I graduated. I married an Irish lass and started a family, and when my company opened an office here in Belfast years ago, I came up to manage it and brought the wife and kids. The Celtic Tiger in the south's financial markets never took hold here so the business didn't flourish, and Brexit took a large bite, but it has continued to make a good living for me. I stayed on in the north as our oldest child, my son Brayden, was accepted to study at Queen's University here in Belfast. I didn't want to uproot the girls again either. I've been raising them on my own since their mother left us many years ago."

"You've stayed in touch with Aiden, obviously."

"Only catching up once a year or so, but he called last month telling me how you'd helped him look for his mother last summer after she'd gone missing, and that I should hire you to look for my daughter."

"And why did you think I might be the right person to help you with that, aside from Aiden's recommendation? Aside from that initial email, you haven't given me much info."

"My daughter went missing in California a month ago. Los Angeles, to be precise."

"Ah, okay then. I'm probably the one you want."

"I have, excuse me – had two daughters. Nora was the first. Rowan was the second. She would have been twenty-five this year. Nora died three months before Rowan disappeared." Daniel shook some remaining raindrops from his bushy hair, and then dug further into his pint. His right hand was shaking almost imperceptibly, as he raised his glass.

"What can you tell me about Rowan. How did she end up in California?"

"She was an independent lass, that one. She was still making up her mind what direction she wanted to go in for a career, but she took a semester abroad at the University of California in LA and was going to school there when she disappeared. In part, I think she wanted a change after we lost her sister."

"What do you know about what happened to her?"

"She was on a weekend trip to that island off the coast there, Catalina, with a man she had apparently been dating. He came back from the island, and she didn't. I flew over, of course, and met with the local police immediately. The man she was with, Jonathan Chambers, was interviewed by the police and said she'd gone out in the town of Avalon by herself in the evening and never returned. He reported her missing the next day."

"Did Chambers continue to be of interest to the police?"

"Not as far as I've been told."

"What else did the sheriffs tell you?"

"They said there was some CCTV footage of her walking by the harbor and heading toward the main dock that night, not long after she'd left the hotel. Avalon Sheriff's Station people and your Coast Guard searched for her body for two days even though no one saw her enter the water."

"No evidence that someone had maybe robbed her and was using her identity - phone or credit cards?"

"Nothing. I came home after a week, then went back to LA again a week later. Talked to the police and a few of her school mates and her landlord. All for naught." Daniel coughed into a handkerchief he'd pulled out of his pocket. More to hide his emotions, I thought, than to clear his throat.

"I'm so sorry, Mr. Collins."

"Please, call me Daniel. Your friend Aiden said you knew what it was like to lose someone close. I hope you don't mind that he told me that."

"My little brother went missing after a carjacking when he was nine and I was thirteen. It wasn't until last year that I found out more about what happened. But I don't know what it's like to lose a child. I can't begin to imagine having to deal with that kind of grief."

Daniel smiled briefly, and said, "When you still have one child and a grandchild left in the world, it gives you something to hang onto."

"How has your son held up?"

"He just puts his head down and keeps on. Brayden is teaching now at Queen's. He's married and has a young son. We've stayed very close, and his young wain is a shining light in my world." Daniel smiled, and there was indeed some spark in his hazel eyes at the mention of his grandchild.

He made another attempt at his pint, then put it down quietly on the highly polished bar. "I'd like you to meet with Brayden while you are here. There are likely to be other people to talk to about her – here as well as in LA, to cover some bases that I haven't. He can tell you who they are."

"Thanks, that would be helpful."

"It puts pressure on people to talk to the surviving father or law enforcement, I think. I'm hoping that someone who is not from the police or the family, might have more luck finding answers."

"It does work like that sometimes. I'll talk to whatever friends Brayden can point me to, and those that she hooked up with in LA. If I can get into her world a bit, it helps me guess where to look for a trace of her, or what she might have done."

"You don't leave a stone unturned, your friend in Edinburgh tells me."

"That's the plan. Did you have any relatives or family friends in the States who she might have been in touch with?"

"Not a one. We're all on this side of the water, of the cousins. And there are no grandparents left. I lost my mother ages ago, and my father to dementia last year."

"My father died recently also. He had Alzheimer's. In fact, that was the last time I saw Aiden. He joined me in Boston for the funeral."

The loss of my father, so soon after reconnecting with him following a period of estrangement, was a fresh wound. I don't even know why I brought it up to a new client whom I did not personally know. Maybe because it was there at the back of my eyes, and I was seeing the world through my own recent loss.

"Thank you for reaching out to me, Daniel. It may be that your daughter's body will never be found, but if nothing else, I hope to be able to put some light on what happened."

"Rowan was always the mentally stronger of my two daughters. Nora had problems with depression all her life, as did her mother, and had attempted to take her life even before her mother left. Sadly, suicide was not out of the realm of possibility for her."

"I'm so sorry to hear she had a troubled life."

"We had Nora in counseling and on medications to help with her illness. But Rowan relished life. If Rowan went into the Pacific Ocean that night, I don't think it would have been of her own doing."

"I know that dock in Avalon. I've been to the island many times. There must have been cameras on the dock?"

"There were, according to the sheriffs, but they weren't working. Older cameras and rusted out from the ocean air."

"That's no surprise. How about other cameras?"

"There was a camera at the dock where the Catalina Express comes in, and I was told that was checked. She definitely did not get on the boat back to the mainland that day or any of the several days later that they looked at."

"No credit card charges, I assume."

"No charges on her cards for transportation – or anything for that matter, after the night she disappeared."

"I expect the Express Flyer ticket office has cameras too, they would have checked those also. What did they say about Jonathan Chambers?"

DEEPER SIX

"I didn't find out much about Chambers. The police interviewed him and ruled him out. I wanted to speak with him, but when I called him, he wasn't willing to meet. I think he felt I blamed him for her disappearance. There was no way I could force him to see me."

"Did the police tell you whether they found any red flags with him?"

"Not a lot was shared with me from the police investigation. Held close to their vests, mostly. If you have any contacts there, maybe you can find out more."

"I'll do some background research on Chambers in the public record and see if anything of interest turns up."

Daniel pulled a piece of paper from his inside pocket and handed it to me. "Here's Brayden's contact. He and Rowan were close. He knows more about her time in Los Angeles. He did his best to help us look for clues as to what happened, but we all came up empty handed."

"Thanks, I'll keep you informed, of course."

"I hope you will have more luck than we did. How is your hotel? Aiden said to put you up at the Culloden when you came over. He insisted nothing but the best would do. It's the best hotel in Norn' Ireland."

"It's lovely, thanks. But he's exaggerating, a local B&B would have been fine."

"I've only driven by it, but I'm glad to hear you're comfortable there."

We finished our pints and parted ways, with a plan to touch base again before I left town.

A concert had just finished at the neighboring music hall as I was leaving the barge, and concert goers were starting to stream out of the building and to the car parks. The lights from the hall were reflecting in rainbows on the wet street, and rain was still trying to fall, though making it through the grey clouds only in sporadic, heavy drops. I grabbed a cab in front of the venue and asked the driver to take me to my hotel. He dropped me off at the Culloden. I entered the exquisitely decorated reception and tracked my way through the halls to my first-floor room, where I promptly fell into bed to sleep off my jetlag.

CHAPTER THREE

The Culloden gleamed in the sun as I walked around the hotel after breakfast the next morning around the 12 acres of sculpture gardens with a view of Belfast Lough. The blond Scottish stone façade of the building coupled with the high turrets gave it the intentional appearance of a small but grand Balmoral Castle. It was named after Elizabeth Jane Culloden, wife of the original owner, and passed into the hands of the church in the late 18th Century until about the 1920s.

In more recent times, the Culloden became the favored hotel of rock bands passing through to perform in Belfast. It was sort of like the Hyatt House, AKA the Riot House in Hollywood, but certainly without the tv sets being launched from upper story windows by stoned rockers. And although coincidently located in the Holywood parish of Cultra, seven miles out of Belfast, the Culloden shared little else with the sixties and seventies LA rock culture. The décor was muted and elegant, as were the guests.

In spite of my down jacket, scarf, wool hat, jeans, and boots, donned for a walk down the quiet Cultra roads to the lough, I felt the bone chill of the increasing wind, even though the sun was shining. Northern Ireland was lush, wet, vibrant. I'd been here a number of times, finally venturing north after having been on numerous visits to the Republic of Ireland in past years.

As a newcomer who hadn't set foot north of the border until after the Good Friday Agreement was signed and the border posts abandoned, the North was part of a whole island to me. It was an island of extraordinary scenery, and lovely, musical people, with its wide diversity of beliefs and creeds. There were continuing flashes of sectarian strife in pockets of the North, but even before the hunger-led diaspora or the north-south division, the small patch of ground sandwiched between the North Atlantic and the Celtic and Irish Seas has always been a wild isle. The island as a whole continues to be alive with the push and pull of history, conflict, myth, music, and progress.

The walkway down to the Belfast Lough shoreline wound through acres of green fields down to the rocky edge of the beach. Dogs were fetching sticks in the water at the behest of their wellie-booted owners, and the wind was blowing hard enough to kick up the sand. A ferry was inching its way down the lough along with a few sailboats. I walked on the path along the edge, passing an old red paint-chipped postbox set in concrete. It had Queen Victoria's royal cypher 'VR' embossed on the front. That's how long the postbox had been there, albeit now unused except as a faded memorial to the 63-year reign that ended with Victoria's death in 1901.

Further along the North Down Coastal Path, catching some spray on my face from the waves against the rocks, I walked by a small boat yard with a bunch of sailboats snugly stowed, including some historic Fairy Class and Dragon Class yachts, awaiting their opening race day. The white-faced building of the Royal North of Ireland Yacht Club was just beyond, along with a more modern postbox across the street, sporting Queen Elizabeth's ERII royal cypher. I circled back up the hill to the hotel and waited in the foyer until a taxi appeared at the reception desk's request to take me into Belfast.

The benches outside the huge glass Palm House in the Botanic Gardens adjacent to Queen's University Belfast was where I'd arranged to meet Brayden Collins. He was there waiting for me when my taxi dropped me off, and there was no mistaking he was Daniel Collins' son. He had the same thick black curly head of hair, short stature, and a younger, less lined version of Daniel's face.

"Brayden, thanks for meeting me."

He held out his hand. "Of course, thank you for assisting my father. He is grasping onto hope, maybe illogical, but if we can all get some closure on Rowan's disappearance and hopefully not death, at least we'll know what went down."

I sat beside Brayden on a bench facing the green gardens, with sunshine pulsing through the clouds.

"Your father didn't give me much detail. Maybe you can fill in some of the blanks."

"He finds it hard to talk about it. I expect he gave you the basics – she had gone to Catalina Island with this man Jonathan Chambers. She was dating him while doing a semester at UCLA. They had a hotel booked for the night in Avalon. She supposedly went for a walk by herself after they had dinner in town and didn't return."

"What did Chambers tell the cops?"

"He told the police he had gone out looking for her for hours, walking all around town and asking people if they'd seen her when she didn't answer his calls or texts. He thought she might have ditched him because their relationship hadn't been going well and maybe she'd taken another hotel room. Next day he reported her missing to the LA County Sheriff's

Station in Avalon. They have jurisdiction there as I'm sure you know."

"How had she gotten to the island? Did he have a boat, or did they take the flyer over there to Avalon from San Pedro or Long Beach?"

"He has a power boat. I'm told that they came over that day and moored in the harbor. I don't know any more about it. I think my father mentioned Jonathan wouldn't meet with him and the police didn't share a lot of details of their interview with him, other than that he was not a person that they had any further interest in. I have his address." Brayden handed me a hand-written note with several names and addresses on it."

"Who is Jacqueline?" I asked, looking at his notes.

"Rowan's roommate. She was also going to UCLA. Rowan connected with Jackie to share an apartment in Westwood near the campus. She talked with my father but didn't add much to the story. She said that Rowan met Jonathan at a bar in LA and they'd started hanging out together a couple of weeks before she disappeared. He's older – thirties something."

"Thanks, I'll be speaking with Jackie, and hopefully Jonathan, soon as I get back to LA. Daniel said you'd had some emails with Rowan before she went missing?"

"Yeah, pretty much the usual stuff. She was digging LA Undoubtedly partying a bit. That was Rowan.

Always out for a glass and some good craic. And she was a fair beauty, so she didn't have much trouble attracting suitors. But she wasn't out of control, you know. No drugs or anything like that. She wanted a career. Even before a family."

"What was her major?"

"Political science. She was going in the direction of public service. She would have set them all straight around here. I could see her taking our Stormont government by storm. God knows they could have used her."

"Did you hear from her just before the trip to Catalina, or when she was there?'

"Only about a week before. She just checked in, nothing unusual. Bragged a bit about the weather, you know, it being a lovely, warm California early spring."

"She was right there."

"There's a friend of hers who you might want to talk to on that list – her best friend Gordie. He's actually in the States right now on a job. He's there a lot. I gave you his contact info also. They were close friends. He was really shattered when she went missing."

"Thanks, I'll look him up." Brayden handed me a 4 by 6-inch full length color photo of Rowan. She had long blond straight hair with bangs nearly overshadowing her shining deep hazel eyes.

Her complexion was fair, and she had a slightly non-symmetrical smile. She was wearing red high heels with a casual outfit, jeans torn at the knees.

"This looks like a professionally shot photo."

"Gordie took it. He's a pro photographer. That's what he does in LA On a gig for a UK studio to shoot stills for a film."

I handed Brayden my card. "Please give me a call if anything else turns up. I'll loop you in on my updates to your father. I hope I can be of some help."

"There is something else," Brayden said, looking away toward the university as though consulting his inner censor before speaking.

"Yes?"

"My father isn't aware of it, but Rowan had a stalker." This was my territory Brayden was wading into.

"Tell me what you know," I said.

"There was a man she met while studying at Queen's, Derek Baker. He wasn't a student. Lived in Dublin and was up here visiting and staying with someone. They dated a few times after meeting in a pub, and she wanted no more to do with him, but he kept bugging her. Quite unhinged it seemed."

"What was the nature of the stalking? Was he physically following her or was it on socials?"

"Physically — I don't think he was using social media. And calling her endlessly on her mobile. He staked out her apartment, followed her to restaurants. He didn't hide it. She was frightened."

"Was it reported to the police services?"

"No, she never contacted PSNI. I got him off her back."

"But why not tell her father or the cops?" Brayden shook his head and avoided my eyes again.

"I didn't want either to know what I did to make him back off."

"Ah, okay." I waited for him to elaborate, or not.

"The problem was handled. He returned to Dublin, and I don't know from there, but he never got back in touch with her."

"You don't need to tell me what happened. I can only assume that you scared him off. Apparently, you didn't kill him." Brayden laughed nervously.

"No, I didn't kill him. I wanted to, but I didn't."

"How long ago did this happen?"

"It was two months before she left for LA."

"And that was the last you and Rowan heard from him?"

"Yes. Dead silence after that. He probably went on to scare the crap out of someone else."

"I'll look into him to rule him out. Did he know of her plans to go to LA?"

"She mentioned it to him on one of the first few times they went out, that she'd been accepted for a semester at UCLA. He knew."

"Thanks for filling me in about him. Probably not relevant to her disappearance, but good to know."

"I don't mind now if my father finds out. I'll give him a heads up. I should have told him back then. I was worried about, you know, repercussions in case the guy got nasty. I didn't want to jeopardize my position at the university. Probably doesn't matter now since he didn't pursue any action against me." Brayden shook my hand and walked back toward Queen's.

Before I left the Botanic Gardens, I wandered into the Palms building and marveled at the towering plant life. The air was hothouse humid. Like a rain forest in Belfast.

CHAPTER FOUR

I hitched a cab back to the Culloden, then walked again through the sculpture garden paths and down the hill toward the lough. Instead of returning to my room, I crossed over a couple of streets toward the railroad line and knocked on the door of the red brick station house next to the overcrossing.

"Ah, come in Mackenzie," Conan O'Donnell said, his smile covering much of the territory from one ear to the next under his bushel of gray hair. "I'm so glad you contacted me. It has been too long."

The seventy-year-old Northern Irishman ushered me into the living room of his home, where he'd lived for all 18 years since I'd first met him on a trip to Belfast. Conan walked with a limp, having broken a leg in several places on a skiing holiday to Switzerland years ago. His cozy living room was the original train station master's house, and the adjoining kitchen was at one time the first-class waiting room. It was renovated with mod cons, but still had the flavor of a restored historical structure. There were several black and white photos on the walls showing the original building and a steam engine parked beside it on the tracks.

"What can I bring you to drink, and what brings you to these damp shores, Mackenzie?"

"I'll have whatever you're having, Conan. Wonderful to see you. I came over to meet with a local guy who has a daughter missing, and maybe dead, in California." Conan put a glass beside me on the table and poured us both a scotch.

"And how is the Culloden treating you? You said when you emailed that you're there for a couple of nights?"

"I got in yesterday. Tomorrow I'm heading down to Dublin to follow up a lead there."

"If only you were staying longer…"

"Next trip, for sure I will and there will be more time to visit."

"What can you tell me about your Irish assignment?" Conan was retired from his own investigative firm but hadn't lost interest in what everyone else was up to.

"You probably read about Daniel Collins' daughter, Rowan, who disappeared in California about a month ago?"

"Yes, yes, there were some articles about it in the Belfast Telegram. Very sad. I don't know the man, but from what I read, even before that, he had the tragic loss of another daughter."

"There is something you might be able to help me with, if you have a chance."

"Say the word, of course."

"Rowan was dating a man named Derek Baker not long before she went to California for a semester at the University of California. He's apparently from Dublin, though he was up here for a time. He was stalking her after they'd had a few dates and she shined him on."

"What kind of stalking?"

"Physically following her and ringing her repeatedly on her mobile, though it wasn't reported to anyone in the PSNI, or even her father at the time. If you still have some local contacts, I wondered if you could check whether he had any run-ins with law enforcement here."

"I will see what I can find out for you."

"Here is his Dublin address, although I don't know if it's current, and also the address where he was kipping in Belfast at a friend's apartment when he met Rowan." I handed Conan a piece of paper with the information.

"And what about you, Mackenzie? How is life treating you?"

I laughed. "Still divorced, still living on a boat. And still wishing I lived in Ireland. I guess that about sums it up."

Conan poured us another scotch while we caught up on each other's lives and I promised to come back soon and spend some time with him. I left and walked back to the Culloden to catch some dinner and some sleep before an early train to Dublin the following morning.

As I boarded the train at Belfast City Center at 0900 for the two-hour trip to Connolly Station in Dublin, I got a text from Conan. It was brief, but I felt the nerves spark in my hands when I read it on my phone. Conan's text said that Derek Baker was arrested in Belfast last year for a violent attack on a woman, though not held by the coppers when the victim wouldn't press charges. He ended the text saying, "Look out for that one, Mackenzie."

CHAPTER FIVE

The loughs and riverways,
green hills and seas
sustain me in the search for others,
along dark paths travelled
while seeking proof of their life.
Proof of mine.

Around 11 AM, I disembarked at Connolly Station on the north side of the River Liffey and took a cab for the short ride to the Westbury Hotel to check into my room. Dublin was breezy and cold, but dry, with a March wind coming in from Dublin Bay. The address Brayden had given me for Derek Baker was a flat just outside of downtown closer to the bay. After grabbing some lunch at a take-away on Dame Street, I took a cab to his last known address in Parkmont Square. I was dropped off in front of a well-kept building, half brick, half stucco. I rang the bell and waited only a minute before it was answered by a twenty-something Caucasian man dressed in wrinkled fatigues, with close shorn greenish hair.

"Looking for Derek. Is he around?" I got a blank stare, as though the man was wondering if I really asked that question or whether he imagined it.

"Ah yeah, I mean, no. Used to share the flat, but not now," he said finally, maybe figuring I didn't look like a cop or a collections agent, so nothing he said could potentially be used against him.

"Will he be back here, do you know?"

"Ah, he's in the USA. Went for some kind of work. Don't know much."

"Any idea where in the States?"

"Yeah, LA, I think. Last I knew. Not one to stay in touch unless you owe him money. Don't have his address or anything, sorry can't help."

"Have you got an email for him, or a phone number?"

"Nah. Except I know he was working for some tech company. Doing something or other with code."

"Did you happen to know Rowan Collins? He was dating her awhile back." My question was followed by a blank stare and a shake of his head.

"Well okay, thanks anyway. If you think of anything else, I'm at the Westbury Hotel one more day. Mackenzie Brody."

"Yeah, right," he said, backing away inside and closing the door. I walked over to the main street intersection and called up a ride with my taxi app to take me back to the hotel. I had only one more day to kick around Dublin before my flight home. I made a call to Daniel Collins to let him know I was leaving the following morning and would keep him updated on my progress.

After lunch at the hotel, I walked around St. Stephens Green in the early afternoon sun. Trees were still drinking up the evening's rain, and the grass on the green was moist and spongy. I made my way over to Trinity College on foot, becoming aware that I was being followed. I occasionally looked over my shoulder from habit, and the man who seemed to be following the same track as myself drew my attention by his slouched appearance. As far as I could see, he was unkempt as though possibly a rough sleeper, and I noticed he was quite tall and lanky. He must have been some good inches over 6 feet. When I got a better look at him as he was crossing the street in my direction, his face was that of a white, young man with a few days' growth of beard.

He gained on me as I continued walking, and assuming he was just going the same direction, might think he knew me, or some other innocent reason, I didn't get worried. I couldn't think of any reason that I might have someone on my tail in Dublin.

Off the road past the university, I turned into a side street and waited at the back of one of the shops for him to catch up, so I could get the measure of him and see if he was on my tail. When he stopped in front of me, he grabbed my shoulders and slammed me against the brick wall in the recess of a building. It happened so suddenly that I didn't have time to react.

"What the fuck are you wanting from me?" he said. "I have nothing to tell you."

"What the fuck are you talking about?" I said, when I'd caught my breath. He released my shoulders but continued to block my exit.

"I don't know who you are, mate" I added in a more conversational tone, hoping to calm him down.

"Rowan. You were looking for me about Rowan." His brown eyes were straight on me, and the intensity of his stare was fit for a zombie movie close-up.

"Ah, so your roommate lied that you were in the States."

"He didn't lie, I was in America. I'm here now."

"I get that. So maybe if you stop threatening me, we can have a chat."

"Like I said, I have nothing to tell you. Stay off my fuckn' back."

"I just want to know when you last saw her. Was it in LA?"

Derek Baker whipped his arm across my face with such force that it spun me around and I fell, landing on my side on the pavement. Derek was gone when I got myself up off the street and looked around.

I remembered that Dublin's Pearse Street Garda Station was a short walk from my location, so I walked to the station. I was met inside the office by a woman officer who took one look at me and kindly suggested that, if I did not need immediate medical attention, she'd escort me to the ladies to clean up my face. I washed the dirt off my face in the ladies' sink. Failing to see any major injury, I figured the rash on my cheek from Baker's jacket sleeve would wear off soon enough.

In lieu of an incident that qualified as a serious crime, I had a five-minute audience with someone from Community Engagement, then filled out a form. If I'd been thinking straight, I could have dialed their 999 emergency number, which would have gotten more of the Garda's attention. As it was, I think the community safety officer figured I'd had a minor altercation with some known individual or a blind date while on holiday from the States, being a feckless American tourist. I could have showed her my Irish passport, since I was a dual American-Irish citizen, but I didn't feel like elaborating on my situation. Further involvement with law enforcement would have taken up the rest of my day. I had other things to do, especially now that I knew Derek Baker was in Dublin and he was sensitive on the topic of Rowan Collins.

"He's in Dublin, Conan," I said into my mobile phone when I'd gotten back to the hotel. "Derek Baker. I just had a brief audience with him. His roommate at the address you gave me said he was in LA, then Baker followed me from my hotel and cornered me in the street here."

"Are you alright, Mackenzie?" Conan said.

"Fine. Just a scratch."

"And you reported it to the Garda?"

"I gave them the gist. But I didn't want to be there all day. Have you a contact here in the south who might be able to track down more about him while I'm back in LA? I'm flying out tomorrow morning and I can't postpone getting back to LA."

"Yes, my friend Cara McKean. She is a top-notch investigator, been in the business for ages, and isn't far from Dublin. I'll text you her number, and I'll call and tell her she'll be hearing from you."

"Thanks, Conan."

"Stay out of trouble, Mackenzie."

"I'm not here long enough for any decent trouble. Next time though."

CHAPTER SIX

Cara McKean of McKean Investigations said she'd meet me at Grogan's at half four. I made my way over to South William Street where the pub is located not far from my hotel. Thriving, even after the loss of its much-respected co-patron, Tommy Smith when he died in 2000, the pub continues to exhibit the work of local artists, and never takes a cut in their sales. I took a seat at a small table against an interior wall covered with paintings, where we'd be out of others' ear shot. When Cara came in, she picked me out easily enough, as I was the only other woman on her own in the bar at that moment.

Cara was a petite, mid length red haired, barely thirty-something Irishwoman in stylish attire. Her outfit consisted of a short black pseudo leather jacket, red silk scarf, tight black jeans, and deep red ankle-high Docs. I immediately wanted her entire outfit.

"Who is the man you're looking for?" She said, getting right down to it after we'd each acquired a pint of the local.

"His name is Derek Baker," I said, and filled her in on as much as I knew about him and his relationship to Rowan Collins.

"Conan found that he had an arrest record last year for assault on a woman in the North. That's all there was to it – charges weren't pressed. I'd like to know if he has a paper trail here and details of his trip to Los Angeles. Whether he was there when Rowan went missing is the main question."

"It may take getting close to him or one of his friends, but that's not a problem, if I can find an entrance."

"I've already blown any cover I might have had with him, and as a local you have the advantage, of course. But you need to be careful. He has a temper. I'll arrange for Daniel Collins to pay your invoices directly," I said, as she handed me her business card.

I parted with Cara an hour later after a couple more pints. I headed back to the Westbury rather later than I'd planned, as I had an early flight to London and then to Los Angeles.

In the morning, I took a cab to the airport for the short flight to Heathrow, then boarded a plane back to LA with the usual feeling that I was leaving home rather than going home. It was just a career in the States that kept me on the wrong side of the Atlantic Ocean. I buckled in for the ten-hour flight and pulled my headphones out of my carry-on bag to watch a trifecta of movies.

Thus far, almost everything and everyone in this case was pointing back to Los Angeles. There is something about investigating on my own doorstep that is more difficult for me than working a case further afield. Maybe LA is crowded with my own memories of having lived in Southern California for twenty years, making it hard to see life there without preconceived notions about people and places. I tend to let my guard down because I assume I know my turf intimately. This case was destined to shake up my mind set about LA, including the amount of trouble I could get myself into close to home.

CHAPTER SEVEN

My floating home in Marina del Rey was bequeathed to me in a divorce settlement from Peter Girard. He'd owned the 45-foot power boat with twin inboard engines when I met him, but I was the one with the driving urge to be on the water. He was a commercial pilot with a preference to be in the air, so other than the occasional cruise together to Catalina or up to the Channel Islands off Santa Barbara, I'd spent more time on the boat than Peter. After we split, it became my refuge from the chaos of Los Angeles, from the loss. I put a bunch of my stuff and a few pieces of furniture in storage nearby and made the boat my home and home office.

I walked down the dock to the boat after parking in the lot next to the marina and stepped over the gunwale into the aft cockpit. My usual seagull visitor, Nigel, was sitting on the adjacent dock, eyeing my arrival with the anticipation of a treat. I unzipped the canvas covering the boat's helm, stepped down into the cabin and threw my bag down on the salon couch. The accommodations were tight but cozy. It was all I needed since I traveled so much. I got settled in and fell asleep in the V berth before I'd even had a chance to cook dinner.

UCLA with its diverse student population roaming about campus and its evocative 5-acre Franklin D. Murphy sculpture garden, was my favorite college campus to visit. The aerial photograph department at the campus, which had collections of historical photos for much of California, was a place I often visited when I was working on environmental pollution cases. You could sometimes find low level aerials of an industrial site showing where the chemicals were stored, and even showing evidence of where chemical waste was dumped, which was very useful in determining who spilled or dumped what and when. The ultimate goal was figuring out who was going to pay to clean up the resulting groundwater contamination.

Rowan Collins' UCLA roommate, Jackie Hori, had responded to my call that morning with a text, saying to meet her in the sculpture garden at noon. She showed up on time, lugging an overstuffed backpack filled with books. Education was not all accomplished on a tablet - yet.

"I had a great time with Rowan when we roomed together. We were off campus – an apartment in Westwood. I didn't know her for long, but she was awesome. I am devastated that she's gone," Jackie said, setting her backpack down and taking a seat beside me on the grass.

"How long did you know her?"

"A few months. The school's student housing people put us together for rooming when she arrived from Ireland."

"What do you remember about her social life and who she hung out with?"

"We were both pretty focused on our classes and didn't have much social time except going out to dinner and bars on occasion. That guy Jonathan that she started seeing was the only guy I remember her dating."

"Do you remember how they met?"

"It wasn't on campus. He wasn't a student. She met him at a bar. He drove a truck for his father's business. Jonathan turned up at the apartment a couple times with this huge tanker truck. I remember because there was nowhere to park it. Parking is at a premium around here."

"Do you remember the name of the company?"

"Yeah, the name was printed on the side of the truck. Chambers Environmental Disposal. Rowan made a joke about him carting her off to the dump."

"What kind of guy was he, if you got to spend any time around him?"

"We hung out together a couple of times. He was older than Rowan by a few years, I think. I don't really know what she saw in him. He seemed a bit pushy. But he was a looker, I'll say that. Rowan said she had a soft spot for anyone who looked like James Dean. She was an old Hollywood movie buff."

"Sorry for all the questions, Jackie, I know it's a lot." She shrugged her shoulders.

"Anything I can do."

"What do you recall about the trip she made with him to Catalina when she disappeared?"

"I was away that weekend visiting my parents in San Francisco, so wasn't in on much of it. I'd left on Thursday. She said she was leaving that Friday to the island for the weekend with Jonathan on his boat. Supposed to be back Sunday. She didn't show and when I got back Sunday night with no Rowan there, and her not answering her cell, I figured they'd stayed an extra day."

"When did you start thinking something was wrong?"

"It was on Monday. I started getting really worried and alerted the school that she hadn't turned up and still wasn't responding to calls or texts. A couple days later the cops came by and looked over her room and asked some questions. I met her father when he came over, and he came back again after that and cleaned out her room. It was awful." Jackie's eyes were filling up, and she stopped just short of a sob, leaning forward so that her jet-black shoulder-length hair covered part of her face.

"I am so sorry. As I said when I called, I met with her father and brother in Belfast. I hope I can turn up some new info at least. And please call if you have any other details about her or Jonathan, or anyone else she might have gotten to know here, that you think might be useful to me."

We parted ways, with Jackie heading to a class while I headed back to the parking structure. Jonathan Chambers hadn't answered my initial phone call to him, but as I was turning onto Hilgard Ave and preparing to take a left on Sunset to the 405, I got a text message from him saying to come by his apartment. I'd run some preliminary database research on him before setting out that morning, and there wasn't much of a paper trail on him. He was in his 30s, appeared to live alone in a rental property, and was employed at his father's waste disposal business as Jackie had confirmed. The criminal litigation record in LA county did not show any arrest or convictions for him.

The only civil litigation that showed up in online indices for LA Superior Court was a case several years earlier where it was alleged his father's company had reneged on a contract to provide transportation services to a building contractor, and he was named as a defendant along with Chambers Environmental. According to the online case docket, the parties settled before trial.

CHAPTER EIGHT

The soft shades of afternoon light spear the
streets and jut through the iron staircases
of the buildings
in this false city.
Amidst this tangle of back lot sets,
I stand on the border,
like a quiet watcher.

Jonathan lived in Venice about 5 houses back from
the beach in an area that was steadily becoming
more gentrified. Despite the astronomical prices
of houses and condos in the area, Venice was still
a mixed bag. The beach neighborhoods hosted
throngs of humanity, especially in the summer
months with tourists, locals, homeless, skate-
boarders, runners, petty criminals, dog walkers,
buskers, and more homeless all sharing the turf.

I rang the doorbell of his ground floor apartment
after getting lucky finding a spot for my car a block

away. You had to have a parking angel to park in Venice; mine was thankfully on duty. Jonathan answered and let me in, then walked in front of me into the kitchen. He was, indeed, a dead ringer for James Dean.

"Have a seat," he said, pointing me to a stool at the kitchen bar counter. He pulled up beside me on another stool. He swaggered slightly in his walk, moving with fluid grace, as though he knew he looked like a 1950s movie star. The creases in his brow cast a shadow over his eyes. Jonathan looked older than his thirty years as he was contemplating my presence.

"You representing the family? Not sure I should be talking to you."

"Yes, I met with Daniel Collins in Belfast, and he has asked me to help find out more about Rowan's situation here and what might have happened. I'm a private investigator, not an attorney. Or a cop."

Jonathan's shoulders relaxed only slightly, but he seemed to be making an effort. "She was a gem, Rowan. I can't believe she's gone. I'd only met her recently, as you probably know. We'd had about five dates." As he spoke, Jonathan fiddled with a small gold cross that was hanging around his neck on a chain. He sighed and looked around the kitchen. "Can I pour something for you? I have beer or water."

"Nothing thanks. Live here by yourself?" The kitchen was neat with everything put away or in its place. Not a scrap of food on the counters. Either Jonathan was a very tidy man, or he had help.

"Yeah, I don't like to have roommates. They make a mess." Jonathan stood up and walked to the fridge. "I'll have a beer, if you don't mind."

"Yeah, no problem. Would you mind telling me how you met Rowan?"

"At a bar in Westwood, near the university. I was there with a couple of friends and struck up a convo with her when I heard her accent. I've been to Ireland a couple of times to visit cousins. My grandfather was from Galway. They had a big family."

"How did the trip to Catalina come about?"

"I have a boat that I keep in a slip in Redondo Beach harbor, a half hour down the coast from here. I go over to the island pretty often, grab a mooring in Avalon Harbor or throw the hook down in Two Harbors to do some snorkeling. My family has a business there too."

"What boat do you have? I know a bit about them. I live on a boat in the marina."

"It's an older fishing style boat, a Bertram if you know them. She's a forty-footer."

"Good boats. The older ones hold up well." Jonathan nodded and kept talking.

"Rowan hadn't gotten a chance to visit the island yet in the time she was here studying, so she was keen to go. We went on a Friday. Got there in the late afternoon to Avalon. It was cold and not too many tourists that time of year, so there was no shortage of hotels. We stayed at a small place up the hill from the harbor where I'd been a couple of times before with friends when they didn't want to sleep on the boat."

"What was the name of the hotel?"

"The Avalon Inn. I told all this to the cops."

"Right, thanks for going through it again."

"We had dinner at a restaurant along the water and got into a disagreement. Not sure what the deal was with her, but we have some differences of opinion about drinking. She didn't want me having a few drinks. I wasn't expecting that. She liked to have a couple herself. But she said she didn't like me when I'd had a few. Didn't appreciate 'the way I became,' she said. I don't know that I became anything, but I like my drink on my days off."

"Where did you go after dinner?"

"Back to the hotel. She said she wanted to go out for a walk on her own, while I stayed in and had another beer. I fell asleep and woke up about midnight. She still hadn't come back. I walked down to the harbor and around downtown looking for her. Figured she'd grabbed another hotel room or made friends in a bar and would show up later. She wasn't answering her cell, it was just going to voice mail."

"At what point did you notify the sheriff's office on the island?"

"First thing in the morning when I woke up and she was still missing in action. I spent the next couple of days hiking all over the island and asking people if they'd seen her. The cops were doing the same, even though they probably thought she'd just taken off with someone since we'd had an argument. Someone remembered seeing her standing at the rail on the main dock about 11:00 the night she disappeared. A camera in town showed her walking by the harbor and heading toward the dock. That was it. No other leads. She didn't buy a flyer ticket back to the mainland. Coast Guard helped looking for her, and the guys who work on the docks - everyone was helping to search for her, even though she was an adult and there was no crime involved."

"I know it's difficult when an adult goes missing and there is no evidence of foul play. It can take some time for it to be established that they're actually missing."

"Yeah, when she didn't show back up on the mainland and wasn't using her phone or credit cards, it really started to look bad. I'm sorry I didn't want to meet with her father when he came over, but my dad said I shouldn't talk to anyone but the cops."

"What kind of business is it that your father runs? You work with him, right?" I knew the answer ahead of time but wanted to keep him talking.

"Waste management. Dad has been in that business forever. Gets hired by companies in LA to pick up their junk and haul it to a landfill. We also have a barge that picks up the trash from Two Harbors and brings it back to the mainland."

"Do you work out of Avalon also?"

"Avalon has its own dumpsite, so the company just runs a few trucks there. I started driving one of the LA trucks while I was in college. I went to community college in Santa Monica and wanted to go into engineering, but it was good money driving for my dad, and he wants me to take the company over eventually."

"Did your father get to meet Rowan while you guys were seeing each other?"

"We had a dinner with him and my mom at their house in Long Beach once. And we stopped by the yard before going to Catalina because I had to pick up something for the boat, so we saw my dad those times."

"You mean Chambers Environmental equipment yard?"

"Yeah, it's in Long Beach. Where we keep the trucks."

"I'm sorry, Jonathan. It must have been really awful for you to lose her so early in the relationship, and on your watch too."

"Yeah, my watch. It was awful. Fucking bad. Part of me is angry at her for whatever happened."

CHAPTER NINE

I left Jonathan's and headed to see Gordon Tamler, Rowan's best friend who was in the LA area on a photo shoot. I was musing over the interview with Jonathan Chambers as I drove. If I was expecting to sense something onerous from the interview with him, it didn't happen. As supposedly the last person to see Rowan he would have automatically been a suspect in her disappearance, but there was no apparent motive. Unless he was convicted for some transgressions out of state that would not have shown up in my online research, he seemed pretty clean. The cops didn't see him as a likely perp, or they would have dived deeper on him.

I could see why Rowan was attracted to him. He gave the initial impression of an okay guy with a good job and a boating hobby, though maybe a heavy drinker. I had to admit to myself that I had wanted him to look or act unseemly, or to give the impression that he was harboring a horrible secret. None of the above was the case, on the surface at least. I wondered how good an actor he might be.

Gordon Tamler was working on a soundstage at Sony Studios in Culver City, fifteen minutes inland from Marina del Rey. He answered his mobile when I'd called earlier, and we'd set up a time to meet at the bar of the Culver Hotel. The 1920s ten-story landmark was as famous for reputedly being lost in a poker game by former owner Charlie Chaplin to John Wayne, as for hosting the entire munchkin cast during filming of the Wizard of Oz. Rumor had it that the munchkin actors got up to all sorts of mischief there.

Gordon told me to expect a white guy with straight brown hair, height of nearly 6 feet, dressed in blue jeans and a black jean jacket, mid-thirties, with no tattoos. As he sat down beside me on the patio of the Culver Hotel, I assessed that his description was spot on except for the tattoo. I could see some ink on his wrist, since he had the sleeves of his jacket folded back a few inches. A small Celtic cross.

"No particularly visible tattoos," he said, sitting next to me and catching my glance at his wrist. "Nice to meet you, Mackenzie."

"You as well, Gordon. Thanks for taking the time."

"Gordie, for short. We're on a break right now with filming, but even if I was in the midst, I want to help in any way I can. Rowan and I were close, as Brayden probably told you."

"When did you last see her?"

"I got together with her just before she came over to the States, then I saw her on one of my US trips just before she went missing. She emailed and we spoke on the phone several times those first few months she was here, and even when we met up here, she had nothing extraordinary to report. She seemed happy."

"Did she tell you anything about Jonathan Chambers – about dating him?"

"She said something about having met a guy, but no details. I know she was mostly focused on her classes. I think he needs to be looked at very closely though. I'm glad you're here and can help with that."

"Why do you feel he needs scrutiny?"

"She called me after their first date, saying he was a bit odd. She said he asked some intrusive questions. Next time she mentioned him, she'd gotten more comfortable with him."

"Did you have any contact with him after she went missing?"

"Not directly. I know the cops didn't pursue him."

"You're about ten years older than Rowan?"

"Seventeen years difference. We met when she started her studies at Queen's. I'd gone back there to do some more studies after being in the work force for a while. We were best suited to friendship because of our age difference, so we didn't date, but we got close. We were like siblings, really. We confided in each other. We hung out a lot."

"Your accent sounds English. Were you born in Ireland?"

"Born in Devon and raised there until I was about 8, then my father brought the family to Belfast when he was offered a job in the north. I was hoping I'd mostly lost my English accent. You've a keen ear."

"How long are you here for?" I asked.

"Another few weeks. It's not my first trip here. I've been up the coast to wine country and down to San Diego. Did a couple of shoots for a UK travel magazine. One place I haven't been is Catalina."

"How are you on boats?"

"I'm good. Did a lot of sailing at various times on holidays in Europe. A friend of mine chartered a sailboat in Croatia last year. I joined him for a couple of weeks to sail around the islands."

"Beautiful country. On my list to go soon."

"Anytime you want to charter a boat, I got good at weighing the anchor at least."

"I want to go over to Catalina to look around. If you have time and want to join me, I'll take the Flyer over the day after tomorrow and stay a night in Avalon.

I'd take my boat, but she needs some engine work."

"Sure, I'd love to join you."

"I don't know if I can accomplish anything there, but I want to talk to a couple of the staff who work the shore boats to see if they remember anything. I can send you the info on the hotel, if you want to reserve a room at the same place."

"That would be great."

A jazz trio was setting up in the corner of the interior bar as we finished talking, so we moved to a table inside and ordered food and wine to stay on for the music. Gordie was turning out to be pleasant company.

CHAPTER TEN

When I got back to my boat that evening, Peter Girard, my ex-husband, was standing on the dock. This happens sometimes. Our post marital relationship was going fairly smoothly two years after the divorce, in spite of my residual anger about him having taken up with another woman on one of his layovers. They don't call it that for nothing, with commercial airline pilots.

"Hey Peter," I said. "Did you just get here, or are you keeping Nigel company?"

"Just arrived, Mac. I hope you're not feeding that bird. You shouldn't encourage them or give them people food," he said. The seagull was posing quietly on the adjacent dock.

As is usual, Peter was looking good in his pilot uniform, six feet tall and handsome, with a lot of hair. It was cut short for the job but had a bit in the front that repeatedly fell down over his eyes. He had a habit of pushing his hair back with his hand, in a somewhat cinematic gesture. I never figured out if he was being purposely charming, or if it just came naturally.

"Yeah, so you always say. The occasional scrap of sushi. He quite likes that," I said.

"He?"

"He's the bigger of the two. Nigella is his mate. Sometimes they come to the dock together. They've been visiting all year." Peter looked at me and shook his head. He was so rooted in reality, and math, and points of the compass, and whatever else. The 'whatever else' had at times turned out to be the other woman. He never totally understood where I was coming from - my imagination sometimes being my guide on the way to the facts.

"Come in the cabin." I stepped over the gunwale into the cockpit, then unzipped the canvas protecting the helm from the occasional Southern California winter rain and unlocked the cabin door.

Caerleon, as I named the boat after Peter transferred her into my name when the divorce was final, was a 45-foot Tiara Sovern express yacht with room to sleep several friends. She was 15-years old, but in immaculate condition. I named her after the legendary seat of King Arthur in Wales for reasons I can't explain.

Caerleon's V-berth held a queen-sized bed, and the guest stateroom aft of the galley had two twin berths. The galley was open to the salon area and had a full-sized fridge and just about everything else one could need for the casual chef. With teak and holly sole flooring under a varnished teak salon table, and couches that converted into another double bed, she was well equipped. She had two heads, the master having an enclosed shower, and there was a small, stacked washer/dryer and air conditioning. Her engine room housed twin Volvo Penta diesel engines that were 370 horsepower per side, giving her a total of 740 horsepower to push her 28,300 pounds to a comfortable cruising speed of 22 knots. With the throttles all out, she'd hit 28 knots, and with her 15-foot beam, she handled the waves like a charm.

Caerleon was my dream boat, which was why I took her instead of the Santa Monica condo in the divorce agreement. Fool that I am. But sitting at the helm of Caerleon, a large 'destroyer' style steering wheel in hand and cruising the coast toward Malibu with a pod of dolphins playing in my wake, was more than I could ask from life.

I loved sailing too, but the power end of things afforded more live-aboard space for my present life where I traveled frequently and didn't want a mortgage. I could also get to Catalina Island in about 90 minutes under power, versus 6 hours under sail. Nothing on the water, however, was any less maintenance than owning a house. Instead of having

gardeners and plumbers, you employ engine me-
chanics and plumbers, because the engines always
need some kind of work, and the fridges are always
breaking down.

Peter sat down at the salon table. "I need some
investigative help, Mac."

"You know I won't work for friends and especially
ex-husbands. It can get too complicated. I can refer
you to one of my PI colleagues whom I'm sure would
do a bang-up job on whatever you need done."

"This is different. I don't want to bring anyone else
in on it. I've got a problem."

"What, Peter? You can tell me about it and maybe
I can suggest something, but I can't take it on."

"It's a case of identity theft. Someone is using my
identity and it's creating havoc. My credit score has
been trashed and I've got creditors calling me for
things I didn't sign up for, but that's not the worst of
it. Someone used a fake ID at an airport in my name
last week to get through security into the terminal."

"The police are helping?"

"There isn't anything the cops can really do except
file a police report. Meanwhile every move I make
must be double checked."

"Any idea who or how it happened?"

"No. It could have been anything, even back to
when a massive hack some years ago swooped up

everyone's identifiers who had ever been issued a US government security clearance. Remember, I had secret clearance at one time for some flight simulator development I did for the DoD."

"It could be a state actor or just someone who happened to hack into DMV records or some such and saw an opportunity to sell your info."

"Right. The problem is cleaning up the mess. If I could have you look into it, I might be able to fend off some of the future complications."

"None of your IDs, cards, or phone got waylaid?"

"Nope."

"You haven't used your ATM card and pin at a gas station instead of a credit card?"

"Nope, not since you did that case where some station owners were using an intercept device to capture the pin numbers."

"You haven't been dating a woman with a foreign intel background?" Peter smirked at that. But I wouldn't have put it past him.

"You must have already contacted your bank and put credit freezes on all three credit companies, changed all your passwords?"

"I've done everything I can think of and taken all the steps the bank and card vendors and cops recommended. And it looks like my identifiers were used by multiple people trying to get credit, so my info was likely being sold on the dark web. Not unusual for criminal gangs to get involved, so I'm told."

"You're going about all the right remedies. There's nothing else I could do for you."

"Could you just run some database and see who the fake addresses go to that were added to my credit report?" I stared at Peter. Everything in my being was telling me not to consent to it.

"Alright, I'll do that much. But you'll have to officially retain me to have you as a client. It has to be in writing. With an advance. You know I can't run any of my subscription PI databases without a client relationship formalized in stone. I could be audited for those protocols anytime."

"Agreed, Mac. No problem. Send me a client engagement letter and I'll sign and send it back. And give you an advance. And one more thing…"

"What? I can't believe I agreed to this," I said.

"It's not a foible to help out your ex. We're ex partners, not ex friends," he said.

"The word foible comes from the French for the weakest section of a sword, from the mid-section to the tip. I think that applies here," I added.

"You would know that." Peter laughed. "But listen, there's another reason you should look into this. Since you were using my last name in some instances while we were hitched, even though you never officially changed your surname, your identity may get compromised also."

Peter was right about that, of course. I hated when he was right, and he pointed it out.

"I haven't had any indication that someone has hijacked my ID, but yeah, it's worth checking it out. I'm sorry. I don't mean to give you a hard time."

"Here's your advance." Peter put a ten-dollar bill on the table.

"You're kidding me, right?" He went back into his wallet and pulled out a fifty.

"You're such a cheapskate."

"Okay, Mac, whatever it costs, just let me know. I've gotta go. I have a flight to Denver. Thanks a million."

The man I adored until I convinced myself I didn't anymore, got up and left. Sometimes or maybe every time I saw him, I still felt the aftershocks of how hard the earth rattled under me when we broke up. I do not know why I caved to do some research for him, because I really didn't want that much to do with him. But this was my pattern in relationships. I didn't see the harm in helping him, as long as the business protocols were followed. I couldn't see what was coming.

CHAPTER ELEVEN

We leftover souls,
languid in our human condition,
are judged by how we stack up
against the gods and the muses.
They watch us watching the clock,
knowing, unlike us,
when it's time.

The next morning, I took an initial stab at Peter's identity theft problem by running a report on him using one of my PI databases, looking for anomalies. There were two addresses that hit on his report which I knew were not associated with him. Both were in Compton, California. When I reverse searched the addresses, they went basically nowhere. I dug further with a quick pass at real estate records, and found the parcels for those addresses, which led me to recorded property documents showing that they were presently vacant lots. It was possible that some person or persons had used those addresses in an attempt to get credit or a loan in his name or switch one of his accounts or cards to a fake address. Further research would have to wait while I focused on Rowan Collins. I sent a quick update email to Daniel and Brayden Collins and headed out the door.

I drove to Long Beach to meet Gordie Tamler at the berth of the Catalina Express for the cruise to Catalina Island, which would take a little over an hour. I parked my car in the lot and walked over to the ticket office to claim my reservation. Gordie was already there, wearing a vest with many pockets over a puffer jacket, carrying a backpack and a beat-up canvas camera bag. He looked like a state-of-the art nature photographer.

"I hope we see some American bison," he said.

"Seeing buffalos will require a ride around the island. They're big and they're fast, so stalking them on foot is not recommended."

The bison herd was scattered over the hills, but it wasn't unusual in the island's interior to catch sight of one of the vestiges of a 1920s Hollywood film. Point being, if you leave a few American bison of opposite sexes on an island after you've ferried them over for staging a western film, you will eventually have a herd. I wonder if William Wrigley, Jr., one time owner of the island, envisioned having up to

600 buffalo on his island. The numbers were kept to 150 in current times for the benefit of the island's ecosystem and the herd's well-being. The ultimate irony to me was not that you could drink Kalua and vodka spiced 'buffalo milk' at most of the island's bars, but that buffalo burgers were also served. That just seems wrong.

We settled in on the Flyer in the interior lower deck seats, since the March weather was brisk, and it was windy, not conducive to the open upper seating. The crossing was uneventful other than passing a couple of heavily laden container ships that were steaming along in the designated traffic lane heading toward Los Angeles-Long Beach Harbor. There was not a dolphin or whale in sight. We approached the Avalon Harbor dock and disembarked as soon as the vessel was secured. The harbor was about half full of power and sailboats at moorings.

"Small seaside town with a pavilion. Reminds me of Brighton, except of course our Royal Pavilion is on the pier, not on the land like yours. It's a casino, yes?"

"It's called a casino, but it's a theatre and ballroom. Sorry, hate to disappoint."

"I don't gamble anyway."

"Me neither. Not with money at least. Let's check into the hotel, then have a look around town."

Our hotel was up the hill from the beach. I'd

booked in at the Avalon Inn where Rowan and Jonathan Chambers had stayed. We rented a golf cart since cars aren't allowed on the island except in particular circumstances, and we drove up to the hotel to register. While I was unpacking in my room, my cell phone rang from an overseas number. It was Cara McKean, my investigator in Dublin.

"Got an update for you, Mackenzie."

"It's late there. Thanks for calling. What have you found out?"

"Your man Derek Baker was in Los Angeles when Rowan went missing. I got friendly with one of his pals, who knew his schedule because they go clubbing together. Derek was out of town when there was a show they had wanted to go to together, so he remembered the date from that."

"What was he doing here? Any news on that from his buddy?"

"Derek has apparently kicked around some software companies. He does some remote computer work for a company named Digital something or other in LA. I couldn't get the full name from his buddy."

"Were you able to get specific dates he was here?"

"No, this guy doesn't know exact dates when he arrived and left LA. It sounds like Derek bounces around, but he was there for a couple of weeks around that time in January."

"Were you able to bring up Rowan's name and see if it rang any bells?"

"I dropped her name, but no indication it struck a chord with him."

"I need a headshot of Baker."

"I have one already, pulled off his socials. Looks fairly current. I'll text it over now."

"Thanks so much."

"One other thing, though, which might make him scared shit of anyone with either a law enforcement or investigative connection or a brain."

"What?"

"According to one of his buddies I talked to, Derek's deep into phishing scams. He's good at it and makes a bundle of bitcoin scamming people online. He might not like having your attention at all. Aside from the fact that he's apparently a psycho stalker, and whatever else."

"Ah, good to know. I'm afraid I haven't trod very carefully around him. I'm taking note."

"I'll let you know if I can develop any more info. And nothing on his arrest record here. A couple of traffic stops is all. He has managed to fly beneath the horizon so far."

"Okay, thanks."

"One other thing. The place he lived in Dublin before you went looking for him went up in flames. I went by the old address, and it wasn't there anymore. There was a Starbucks going up in that spot. I asked around and found out that there used to be flats there. When I asked his buddy about it, he said that Derek owed the landlord a bundle, but got away with it when it burned down. So maybe he's a pyro too."

"Ah Jesus."

CHAPTER TWELVE

I went back down to the hotel reception to speak with the staff and show them the photo of Rowan to see if they remembered her staying there. The manager happened to be at the front desk, a forty-something man in casual clothes who gave no managerial impression, but had the name tag of "Richard, Manager," to prove his status.

"Yah, I remember her because the sheriff came by the next day asking about her and her friend."

"Did anyone mention hearing or observing any arguments between Rowan and her friend when they were here?"

"No. I checked with all the desk and housekeeping staff. No one remembered anything. The sheriff checked their room before we turned it over – the guy was still staying there - and as far as I know, they didn't find anything. I remember that her friend stayed on a couple more days while they were searching the island for her."

"Okay, thanks. There was another person who might have been around at the time, Derek Baker." I pulled out the photo on my phone that Cara had sent.

"I don't recognize the face."

"Can you check the register to see if he stayed at the hotel around the days when Rowan was here?" I asked. "It's Derek without a 'c'."

"I'm not supposed to, but I guess it wouldn't hurt." Richard, the Manager, went over to one of the computers behind the registration desk and punched some keys."

"No one by that name in the system."

"Thanks for looking."

Gordie joined me in reception, and we took the golf cart back down to the main drag by the harbor and returned it to the rental company. We stopped for lunch in one of the harbor cafes and sat outside on the patio.

"We haven't really had a chance to talk, Mackenzie, with that boat ride being rather noisy. How long has it been since you were in Catalina last?" he said.

"A while. Gets pretty chilly in the winter months for sitting at a mooring at least. I was here in the fall. I brought my boat over for a weekend with some friends. Please call me Mac. It's easier."

"Okay Mac. So, you live on the boat?"

"Year round. She's a good size, and I travel a bunch. It's fun and enough space. I love waking up in the morning and feeling the boat sway and the creaking of the dock ramp moving with the tides. And for a space to do some writing. It's good inspiration."

"Not sure I could do a boat habitat for long, but it sounds grand."

"Yeah, it's a different lifestyle for sure. Before I married my ex, I had an apartment in the marina, then he came with a fully furnished condo and the boat. I got rid of a lot of my stuff except a few things in storage. I travel light now. What about you? Do you have a place in Belfast?"

"I have an apartment in Belfast near Queens. I'm on the other side of an 'ex' as well. We split up two years into the marriage when it wasn't working out. No kids, so it was okay. We were young. I was just twenty then, and neither of us took the time to know each other before we married."

"I know how that goes."

"We should have lived together for a while first and figured out if we were compatible for the long term. I've been a bit more circumspect since, in re-lationships at least."

"Same here, I guess you could say. How has it worked out for you to have a career as a photographer?"

"I've been lucky to have a lot of work. It's not easy to make a living at it, but once I got hooked in with the studios, I've done alright."

"That's great. I have the photo you took of Rowan that Brayden gave me."

"Rowan's one of a kind, you know. She has a presence about her that's hard to put into words. She is kind to a fault and compassionate to a fault. Not easily shaken from that perch either. She wanted to go into government after uni, but more the ambassadorship side of things, not elected office. At the same time, she's quirky and fun. No lack of flare, that girl. And she's brave. God, I love and miss her."

"What do you mean she's brave?"

"She's not afraid to try on new things, like traveling to the States on her own to help herself cope with the loss of her sister. Not one to sit around feeling sorry for herself. And she'll do stuff like have a closet full of red shoes. A pair for each day of the week. Heels, flats, boots... she said it was to remind herself to do something different every day - work, hike, dance, whatever."

"I like the red shoes thing," I said.

"What do you think are her chances?"

"When an adult is gone for a month with no contact, that's not a good indicator. I don't have high expectations of finding her alive."

"Christ, Mac." Gordie's eyes were wet.

"The reality is that every day that passes it gets less likely to turn anything up. But I hope to bring some comfort to the family and her friends like yourself, if I just can find out what the hell happened," I said.

"I understand that. But it's bloody hard. She called me her rock, but really, she was mine."

"Just because it's against the odds of finding her though, doesn't mean it can't happen." Gordie smiled and shook his head like he was casting off unwanted thoughts. "You do a lot of this, looking for disappeared people?"

"It has turned into a specialty over time. I've had to search for a lot of people – sometimes as witnesses for litigation, or people who are victims for a class action suit. Sometimes it's people who used to work for companies in a pollution case. Like who dumped it and who's going to pay to clean it up."

"Do you look for criminals?"

"I don't do criminal work unless it's white-collar or pollution. I have no stomach for hard core perps, although I've run across a few. I don't want to know about blood spatter, rigor mortis, and after-death flesh-eating bugs."

"You may have a criminal on your hands here."

"I know. Hopefully with no flesh-eating bugs."

CHAPTER THIRTEEN

We walked down to the main dock at the harbor after lunch, and I spoke to a couple of the guys who ran the shore boats, providing water taxi service to and from boats at moorings for people who didn't have their own dinghies. Neither of the guys who were working recalled Rowan or Derek Baker, but both had recently started and might not have been on a shift at the time. They said I should come back when Sandy was working, since she'd worked the shore boats for several years. I knew her from my Catalina trips, and said I'd come back when she was on duty.

It was obvious that the sole camera on the main dock was inoperable since it was hanging by a wire. As we were walking back from the dock, I noticed a trash truck with a Chambers Environmental sign on the side. It was smaller in size than the usual waste pick-up trucks, probably so it could make it down the cramped alleys of Avalon.

"Huh, Jonathan said they do some trash pick-up here," I said. "I wonder if they have an equipment yard in Avalon as well as the yard they have in Long Beach."

"Let's ask," Gordie said. He walked over to the truck and spoke to the driver in the front seat. The driver was eating a sandwich while pulled over to the side of the main drag.

"Hey, do you guys have a yard here?" Gordie asked.

"At the dump. Do you need to get rid of some stuff there?" the driver asked.

"No, just wondered how things work. I thought maybe you had to ferry all the trash to the mainland."

"Naw, there's an Avalon dump for non-hazardous stuff. We take some trash out of Two Harbors at the other side of the island by boat over to Long Beach, but the only things that go from here by barge are drums of waste oil and that kind of thing to a special dumpsite on the mainland."

"Thanks – sorry to interrupt your lunch," Gordie said.

"No problem."

We walked back over to the waterfront and sat on one of the benches.

"That jives with what Jonathan told me," I said. "I'd like to check out their yard here. Kind of boring for you. Why don't you take a Hummer tour to the interior and see if you can see some buffalo?"

"You're sure you don't want company to the yard?"

"No, you go buffalo hunting. Let's meet up for dinner, how about at the Harbor Café at 6:00?"

"I'll be there, whether I shoot any buffalo or not," Gordie said.

The Avalon dump, where the Chambers equipment yard was located, was outside town. I rented a golf cart and headed that way, after getting directions from the rental agency. I drove past town and along some rough roads, paved but with a lot of sand on them that left the golf cart straining to keep a purchase on the pavement and sent up clouds of dust. I hoped I wouldn't be charged for a full detail of the cart when I returned or reprimanded for taking it on a sandy road.

The afternoon had turned warm and sunny, and a few small lizards skittered off the road, their sun-baths interrupted as I passed. When I rounded the turn in the direction of the dump sign, there was an area enclosed with a chain link fence and an entrance with a sign that said, 'Chambers Environmental.' The gate was open, so I drove in and toward a small trailer with a sign hanging on the front door that identified the office.

There were several trash trucks parked near the building and numerous pieces of equipment that looked like vehicle parts, plus a few open-haul trailers parked on one side of the office. No humans were in evidence until I parked the golf cart and knocked on the office door.

I hadn't really thought through what I was going to say, so I opted for the easiest explanation for my visit, the truth. A man pulled the door open abruptly. He was white, probably in his forties, and a bit overdressed for his supposed occupation. In a suit and tie, he looked like a banker, not a waste hauler employee.

"How can I help you?" he said.

"Is the manager available?"

"You're looking at him. Greg Chambers. There is a website form you can submit for household issues, or a number to call. We don't service any residents here. This is just an equipment center." He looked too young to be the father of Jonathan Chambers. My guess was a brother or cousin.

"I'm not a resident here. I met Jonathan a couple of days ago. You must be his brother?"

"Our father owns the company. I just manage the Catalina end of things. Who are you?"

"Mackenzie Brody. I'm helping the family of a woman who went missing in Catalina a month ago, Rowan Collins. She was visiting Avalon with Jonathan, as I expect you may have heard."

"I know about that. What does this have to do with our company? Are you a cop?"

"Private," I said, reaching into my bag for my wallet and my PI ID card. I held it out so he could see it. He leaned in and squinted like he really needed reading glasses.

"Jonathan mentioned that the firm had some waste collection business on the island, and I thought I would stop by and see if anyone here who was servicing the town might have seen her while she was here."

"The answer is no. Jonathan asked me to speak to the drivers when he was helping to look for her, to see if anyone had seen her. The answer is no." Greg Chambers repeated himself for emphasis, apparently. The tone of his voice was rising in irritation or some other visceral reaction to my question. I found that interesting.

"That's good to know, thanks," I said, dodging his increasingly confrontational posturing.

"You should speak to the LA County Sheriff's office, not my drivers. The only two who were on the job that weekend were relief drivers from Long Beach. They were filling in and don't work here on a regular basis. And Jonathan won't be talking to you again. You can speak to our attorney."

"Right, well no issue there. I'm just trying to help her family figure out what happened to her. Thanks anyways," I said, turning to leave before things got any more tense.

Greg Chambers stood at the door watching me get in the cart, then walked behind me as I maneuvered the cart toward and through the exit. Out of the corner of my eye as I drove the cart around, I saw him pull up a cell phone from his pants pocket and take a photo of me in the cart. He closed the gate behind me with a flourish, slamming it for good measure.

The downhill ride in the cart was easier, and as soon as I hit the paved road, I probably violated the 20 MPH speed limit. It was kind of like driving a little runabout boat, but with brakes, such as they were. I slowed as I got into town and was stopped at a stop sign when the cart was hit suddenly from the rear, pushing it forward into the intersection. An oncoming car barely avoided swiping me from the side. I went flying onto the street and rolled into the gutter against the curb. I heard screeching tires and froze, hugging the curb, waiting for further impact to my body if it was to come. When death didn't come, I rolled over to assess the damage. I couldn't see any blood or feel any pain, I just had a dazed view of the scene and a couple of people running toward me as I sat up.

"Don't move," someone said. "In case you've broken your back."

"I'm okay," I said, "I can get up. Where's the car that hit me?"

"It was a white truck. It backed up and took off. Hit and run," another bystander said.

"Did you see the driver? Get a plate?"

"No, a white pick-up truck is all I saw."

"Doesn't everyone know everyone in this town? There aren't even that many private cars on the island," I said, mostly to myself.

I shakily got to my feet, reaching my hand out to the shoulder of one of my witnesses to steady myself. My head was clearing, which was a good sign. The witness I was presently leaning on was a young woman, who was looking very concerned.

"Could I get your info for the cart rental? They'll want a witness for insurance, and I'll need one, so they don't bill me," I said, looking at what was now a sad excuse for a golf cart. It was totaled, with the back end scrunched in.

"Of course. My name is Maria Sanchez. What's your name?"

"Mackenzie Brody. Thanks for your help."

I reached in the pocket of my jacket for my phone, but it wasn't there. "Anyone see a phone lying around? It must have flown out of my pocket." One of the several bystanders picked something up off the ground and brought it over to me. My phone was also in a sorry state, with the screen cracked. I touched the screen to see if it would respond. No luck.

"Maria, I'll give you my cell number, if you could please leave me a message with your info and what you saw. I'll forward it to the rental company."

"Sure. Let me give you a ride somewhere."

"Let's get the cart over to the side of the road, and if you wouldn't mind taking a couple of photos of it too, that would be helpful." Maria already had her phone in hand and took a couple of shots of the cart and the intersection. Meanwhile, someone rang 911 and reported the incident, which I'd hoped to avoid due to the time law enforcement involvement would take up. Another good Samaritan pushed the cart into a parking spot on the side of the street.

"If you could drop me off at the rental place across from the pier, I'll give them the bad news," I said.

"Are you sure you're okay? There is an urgent care center here. I can take you there in my cart."

"I'm alright. I just want to go to the cart company, get a replacement and go back to my hotel."

"You have a scrape on your forehead. You should ice that," she pointed out. I put a hand up to my head and felt a bump. My head wasn't the only casualty. The cross-body bag I'd been carrying was still attached to my body, fortunately, but not so fortunately, I'd landed square on its bulk. One more location for an ice bag.

Maria held my arm as we walked over to her golf cart. Just as I got on the seat beside her, an LA County sheriff's patrol car, one of the few on the island, pulled up. We spent the next fifteen minutes talking to the sheriff about the hit-and-run while he made notes and got the names, contact details and stories of Maria and the several people who were still standing around to see if I would possibly drop dead, to give them something more to talk about. The cop excused me eventually with an admonition to seek medical help if I showed any signs of concussion, and Maria drove me the few streets over to the main harbor road and dropped me at the cart rental.

"Where's the cart?" the kid asked, who looked about fifteen-years-old, but must have been at least twenty-five, since that's required to drive a golf cart there. I gave him the short version, and he directed me to the office to fill out a form. That took another twenty minutes while the manager debated whether it was a risk to rent me another cart in case I should trash the second one.

"Your insurance company will confirm from witness statements taken by the sheriff that I stopped properly at the sign and was rear ended by a hit and run pick-up truck," I said, impatient with the process as various parts of my body were starting to ache.

I summarily rented another vehicle and drove it up to the hotel. Without a working phone, I couldn't reach Gordie, so I decided to lay low with an ice pack offered by the hotel receptionist until meeting him for dinner in town.

"What happened to you?" Gordie said, when he sat down across from me at the restaurant and observed the red rash on my forehead.

"Uh, hit and run. Golf cart accident."

"Bloody awful, Mackenzie, how did that happen?"

"Rear ended in town just as I got back from Chamber's yard. All I know is it was a white pick-up truck. None of the witnesses recalled anything else. I got thrown to the curb."

"Did you get any medical attention?"

"No, I'm alright, just a bit of bruising. But I think I'll skip the before-dinner wine and go straight to the vodka." Gordie signaled the waiter, and we ordered martinis and menus.

"I hope you won't feel worse tomorrow. Whiplash and that."

"We'll see. Unfortunately, my phone took a hit." I pulled it out of my pocket and showed Gordie the busted screen. He took it from me and fiddled with it. It came to life, although the screen was indecipherable.

"Just because the screen is fried doesn't mean you can't fix it. I bet there's a shop here who can replace the screen. Let's check in the morning."

"How did it go with your search for buffalo?"

"Aye well, I missed the hummer ride, so I kicked around the island a bit. No buffalo, just a few of the island foxes. Maybe next time on the bison."

"You know the Native American Chumash considered the Catalina foxes a sacred animal and a dream helper."

"They are beautiful little animals. Their terrain here reminds me of the coast of Portugal. Similar climates. How did your trip to the Chamber's yard go?"

"I met the yard boss, so to speak. He's Jonathan's brother, Greg. He wasn't keen on my visit. He said Jonathan wouldn't be speaking to me again, and that the couple of guys who worked for the company here on the day Rowan went missing were from Chamber's Long Beach facility. They were subs for the usual Catalina crew."

"You'd think they'd want to help. What's wrong with these people?" Gordie said.

"I don't know. Something's going on with Greg Chambers, but whether it has anything to do with Rowan's disappearance is an open question."

"What about this crash you just had. Suspicious?"

"Another question. I'm wondering how many white pick-up trucks there are on Catalina. Couldn't be too many. It takes years to get a permit for something bigger than a golf cart here. Greg Chambers took a phone photo of me in the cart as I was leaving. Maybe he sent it to one of his guys to intercept me in town, and the hit-and-run was my Catalina exit invitation."

"Could be. If Rowan was taken by Jonathan Chambers, or if they have something else to hide, you might be shaking a dangerous family tree."

"Sometimes it happens, Gordie."

CHAPTER FOURTEEN

On an island wedged between
canyons and sea,
cluttered with promises and history,
the surrounds carry an imbalance
that sweeps like a hawk through its streets,
to hearths, to hearts.

After dinner, we walked back to the main drag and over to the pier. A shore boat was just tying up at the dock, and I recognized Sandy, who was a regular. She was often on duty when I came to the island, when she wasn't running a charter fishing boat.

"Sandy, how are you these days?"

"Hey Mac, nice to see you. I didn't see Caerleon come in. Did you come over on your boat?"

"She's waiting for my engine mechanic. Came over on the Flyer. This is my friend Gordie. Can we talk for a minute?" I said.

"Sure." Sandy finished tying the shore boat lines to the dock cleats and hopped up on the dock.

"Did you hear about a woman who went missing here about a month ago? An Irish woman named Rowan Collins."

"Yeah, I was here that weekend, but didn't hear how it ended. Was she found? Maybe not if you're involved?" Sandy knew the business I was in, and her first question when we ran into each other on Catalina was usually whether I was working on any interesting cases. She knew she'd get the same response every time. I tell her I'm working on an amazing and intriguing case, that I can't tell her a thing about.

"Not found. I'm working for the family to see if I can turn up any more info about what happened."

"You know the sheriff's guys never talked to me. I was expecting they would, but I guess they were busy with the Coast Guard looking for a body. I might have seen her that night, at least I thought it could have been her."

"What do you remember?"

"It was later in the evening. Must have been on Saturday as that was the only shift I was working that week. Jon Chambers, you know him? He's here a lot with his boat Flight Risk, 'cause the family does the waste hauling here. He was with a girl, and they got on his dingy and went over to his boat that was on a mooring."

"Do you remember what time of day it was?"

"It was after dark; I remember that much. I could have been mistaken. It could have been another woman with him. I just remember thinking Chambers had another girl in tow. I've seen him around here with various girlfriends or whatever they are."

"Any recollections about her – height, weight, skin color, hair color, dress?"

"Little shorter than him. Caucasian, average weight maybe, blond, I think. But she had a baseball cap on. Nothing special about clothes. Maybe jeans and a jacket."

"Did Chambers take off in his boat that night?"

"Don't know. I was off at eight, and Marcus took over for me. He's on tomorrow. I can ask him."

"Great, thanks. I can't show you a photo of her tonight because my phone is broken, but I can stop by here sometime tomorrow. What's your schedule?"

"Here all day," she said, picking up a gear bag from the dock. "Marcus is here too. It's starting to get busy, so we'll be running two boats."

"Thanks. I'll come by on the way to the Flyer tomorrow."

Gordie and I walked back to the main street in the fading light, while the numbers of tourists out on the streets was starting to diminish. I wasn't quite ready to part ways with him for the evening and he seemed to know it.

"Stop in for a drink on the way back to the hotel?" I asked.

"I was about to suggest the same. How is your head?"

"Got some ibuprofen in my bag and that should do it, with a vodka chaser." We found an open restaurant a few hundred yards away and went in, sitting down at the bar. After we ordered drinks, Gordie put his hand on my shoulder, then gently rubbed the back of my neck. I almost recoiled from his touch, then caught myself. I hadn't realized how much tightness I had in my muscles from the crash, or how much emotional back-off I had lately to physical contact.

"You need to relax, Mackenzie."

I shook my shoulders, which must have been up around my neck. "That helps, thanks."

"I'm pretty good at a full body massage, if that would help," he said.

I looked at him and laughed. "Nice invitation. I'll give it some thought."

"I'm part English, you know. It's remarkable that I dared to even suggest it. America is rubbing off on me."

"You're doing fine. I'm maybe not so fine. Nothing to do with you though."

"Post-divorce damage?"

"That and a bit of overly cautious investigator, and the fact that you're involved in my current case. It's a nuisance, really."

"If you need to run a background check on me before a massage, I fully understand," he said, laughing.

"Not to change the subject, but I'm wondering if Sandy's recollection is accurate and if it was Rowan getting into Jonathan's dingy with him that night. That would throw a whole wrench into Jonathan's story and mean that Rowan was taken off the island by boat and something happened to her after that. Possibly at Jonathan's hands."

"Do you remember I told you how Rowan is an old Hollywood movie buff? She was obsessed with the story of Natalie Woods' death off a boat in Catalina."

"It was 1981. Another unsolved mystery."

"Someone caused Rowan some pain on this island," Gordie said. There was smoldering emotion in his eyes.

We walked back to the hotel as dusk was descending. The sounds of a small beach town were winding down, and we caught sight of two deer at the edge of the road that skittered off when we got close.

The wind that had picked up before the sun had set slowed down and settled, as it often does. I said good night to Gordie with some regret, torn between my attraction to him, my fear of another relationship, and the potential complications of becoming involved with someone related to the investigation.

When we got down to the harbor the next morning, the wind had increased again, and lines were clanging in a counterpoint song against the masts of the sailboats at their moorings. It was low tide and the air smelled like fish, seaweed and the small sea creatures that clung to the rocks along the shore. We stopped in at a shop on a street running parallel to the main drag and had the screen replaced on my phone, then walked over to the dock to meet Sandy.

"Here's the photo I wanted to show you. This is Rowan." I held out the phone and she scrutinized the picture.

"Pretty girl. Still can't say for sure it was her I saw with Jonathan that night. Could have been, but could have been anyone, really."

"How about this guy," I said, pulling up a photo of Derek Baker.

"Who is he? I do remember this guy because he really pissed me off. One night I caught him trying to steal a boat that didn't belong to him from the dingy dock. He gave me some story or other, which I knew was a load of bullshit, then he took off back into town and I didn't see him after that."

"When was that?"

"That would have been around the same time — can't say exactly when, but I was on for a couple of weeks around the time when the girl went missing."

"Thanks, that's really crucial info about Baker. It's the first time I've heard that he was here on the island."

"Also, I checked with Marcus about Chambers, and he doesn't remember seeing Chambers or his boat that week. Sorry I can't help there."

"Thanks, Sandy, catch you next time I'm over. Hopefully on my boat soon."

The trip back to San Pedro on the Catalina Express was a bumpy ride with the swells hitting 3 to 4 feet, but this time we had a large pod of dolphins surfing the boat's wake for part of the trip. We stayed on the top deck and I watched the exuberant show while Gordie took photos with his zoom lens. I decided to stop in Redondo Beach on the way back and get a look at Jonathan's boat in the Portofino Marina, and Gordie agreed to join me.

After we landed in San Pedro and got back in our cars, I drove north on the 405 to Artesia and west to

Redondo with Gordie following me in his rental car. We pulled into the parking lot, where Jonathan was keeping his boat in a slip in front of one of the marina hotels. Gordie joined me and we walked through an open gate and down the ramp to find his slip. I didn't have the slip number, but it was easy to find, considering the fact that Jonathan was sitting on the gunwale of about a 40-footer that I recognized as a Bertram sport fisher, looking at his cell phone. His boat, perhaps aptly, was named Flight Risk. He put the phone in his back pocket when he saw me.

"Again," Jonathan said, with something between humor and irritation in his voice.

"Thought I'd stop by and see what you drive. Nice looking fisher."

"She's got some years on her, but I've had her for ten and kept up the maintenance. Who's your friend?" he said, looking at Gordie.

"Gordon – Jonathan," I said, gesturing a casual introduction. "What's with the 55-gallon barrels," I added, pointing to the two black, slightly rusty metal drums in the cockpit, which did not appear to be fishing tanks, and they took up almost the entire deck of the cockpit. "That looks like a heavy load to transport."

"Sometimes I bring some drummed waste back from the island and deliver it to our yard here for transport to a landfill. Used oil, that kind of thing." I was skeptical. Having full drums of a hazardous waste sitting on the back of your boat for a 27-mile crossing when the seas could get rough, was not my concept of a good idea. An ocean-going barge with the proper transport license for hazardous waste would be the right ride, not a personal sport fishing boat. I decided to challenge him. It did not go over well.

"I didn't realize one could get a license to transport hazmat on a private boat," I said. Jonathan's lower lip pressed firmly up against his top lip, contorting his handsome mug.

"Not sure what business it is of yours. Is there anything else you want to know?" He stood up in a defiant posture, sticking his hands in his jean's pockets. He was starting to piss me off.

"One of my friends who runs a shore boat on the island remembers you getting into your dingy with a woman the night that Rowan went missing. Got any recollection about that?"

"Your shore boat captain is mistaken. I didn't take the dingy out that night or go back to my boat. I was walking around Avalon looking for Rowan, like I told you and the sheriff."

"Okay, thought you might have run into another friend on the island. I'm not accusing you of anything."

"You should think about leaving well enough alone private fucking dick."

"Right, Jonathan. Good luck with the hazmat. You might want to look into getting a barge with a license before an accident with those drums sinks your boat."

"I'll be sure to do just that," he yelled after us, as we were walking back up the ramp to the parking lot.

"Touchy guy," Gordie said, when we reached our cars.

"This Chambers waste hauling business is looking dicey. I've got some research to do."

"Let me know if I can help with anything at all. We need to nail his ass. You know where to find me," he said.

"Will do, and thanks for coming along to the island." Gordie waved at me as we got into our separate cars.

I drove back to Marina del Rey with the intention of getting on my computer to investigate the paper trail on Chambers Environmental.

CHAPTER FIFTEEN

Nothing could have prepared me for what I found when I got back to the boat at dusk. Caerleon was engulfed in black smoke and flames. She had been pushed back out of her slip, obviously to keep the adjacent boats from catching, and LA County Fire boats 110 and 310 were hitting her with water from both sides. The Sheriff's boat, a Coast Guard boat, and a Baywatch boat were standing by in the channel with lights flashing, and the red lights of a fire engine and the flashing blue lights of several cop cars on the street side were adding to the chaos.

I pulled over and parked along the street, not bothering with the parking garage, and ran toward the open gate at the top of my gangway. I was hollered at and then physically blocked by a posse of two sheriffs and a fireman.

"It's my boat, I have to get down there," I yelled.

"You're not going anywhere near it right now, lady," one of the cops yelled back over the cacophony.

"I have to move my runabout that's right across it before that catches." A burly fireman in full yellow regalia put a hand on my shoulder.

"We've gotten all the boats moved on either side. They are out of harm's way. No wind. This fire isn't going to travel. Stay here where it's safe," he said. I merely nodded and backed away a few paces, leaning against the railing in shock.

The flames that had been shooting up from the back of the boat were getting doused, and black smoke continued to pour into the air. The light breeze was pushing the smoke in my direction, and it smelled like a toxic mix of chemicals. I choked on the soot filled air.

I felt another hand on my shoulder, and turned to see the dockmaster, who I'd known for several years.

"What the fuck, Bill?"

Bill had a hand full of N95 masks and gave me one as he donned one himself. "Here, I grabbed these as I was heading over here. This smoke is bad news."

"Thanks," I said, chocking from my tears in addition to the smoke.

"No telling yet what started this, Mac. There was no explosion, at least not that I heard."

"What do you know?"

"The first thing I heard was when one of the kids from the adjacent apartments came running into my office saying there was a boat fire. The fire department had already been called by one of your dock mates, and before I could even get out of my chair, I heard the fireboats and the sheriff's boat with sirens blazing coming into the basin, and the ladder arriving on the street. Quite a circus."

"Is everyone on the dock okay?"

"No one was even on their boat on your dock when it started. Firemen pushed your boat back out of the slip to protect the neighbors, and a few boaters on neighboring docks were evac'd after they helped get the boats that were closer to it moved. Your Chris Craft was moved over to the 400 dock."

"You know there was no reason for Caerleon to catch fire. Someone has torched her."

"The fire department arson investigator and your insurance investigator will find out, Mac. Those guys can spot arson a mile away."

"She's a total loss," I said, watching the fire die down under the continuing deluge, black smoke still billowing, while the firemen were simultaneously de-watering her with a pump to make sure she wouldn't sink. Tears were stinging my cheeks. I didn't bother to wipe my face.

"Have you got somewhere to stay?"

I hadn't even thought about that. My home was gone, along with my clothes, shoes, galley equipment, a few pieces of cherished artwork and my favorite pair of expensive marine binoculars. Thankfully my important documents like my car's pink slip, family photos, computer back-ups and a few pieces of furniture that I kept from my last apartment were in a small storage unit in the marina. I was running through the list of losses in my head. I didn't answer him right away.

"I have my laptop, and my passport, licenses, and credit cards are in my purse, thank God," I said, without being asked.

"I'll get you set up with a room at the Marriottt, Mac. Don't worry about it. Just go over there when things quiet down here. It'll be under my name."

"Thanks Bill." My eyes kept watering from the smoke and tears. The boat was insured, of course, but I had a special affinity for Caerleon. She was a safe space for me in what had been a difficult couple of years. I had no plan B for housing, or for restoring the peace she'd given me on the water through the loss of a marriage, the death of my father, and the roller coaster ride of the past year that had culminated in a search for my little brother's killer. I exhaled heavily then coughed.

"Who or which agency should I talk to of all these first responders?" I asked Bill, shouting over the cacophony and the mask.

"I'll let them know the owner is here. They'll come to you. Sheriff and Fire will want to talk with you. You don't want to stay until the bitter end of the clean up here, Mac. The air is too foul. I'll tell them how to reach you. Go to the hotel and get yourself a drink."

"Thanks."

"Is there anyone you want me to call for you?"

"No," I said. Several of my close friends were on a trip together to wine country and I had no intention of phoning my ex. He was just another reminder of a loss; besides I hadn't done the research he asked me to do, and I knew he'd press me on it. I stayed at the railing watching the flames die until I couldn't take it any longer. I walked back to my car and drove a few streets over to the hotel and checked in. I took off my mask and acrid smoke-smelling jacket, called room service to order a bottle of wine, then rang Gordie's number.

"Did you get back to the marina okay," Gordie asked after picking up.

"My boat has been burned down to the hull, Gordie. I got back to find her in flames. Good chance it was torched."

"Oh Christ, Mac. Where are you right now?"

"My dockmaster booked me in at the Marriott in the marina. It's a couple blocks from what remains of my boat. I left before the embers were out. Couldn't handle it any longer."

"I'll come over if I can be of any help." The sound of Gordie's hybrid English – Irish accent reminded me of something I couldn't place, something calming.

"Remember that massage you offered? That would help," I said, and hung up the phone.

CHAPTER SIXTEEN

I'm driven to the edge by the story
that burns,
the narrative that begets fire.
I can ache like part of the earth,
trespassed.

Gordie spent the night. I just went with it, not caring about the fact that this was not my usual cautious approach to a date night, or any of the other reasons I probably shouldn't go that far with him. I finally fell into a solid sleep in his arms about two in the morning, and only woke when my phone rang at 9 AM. It was the LA County Sheriff's Department asking me to come to the station to meet with them that afternoon on Fiji Way in the marina. I also had about fifteen texts from various people who'd heard about the fire, and several from Peter asking if I was back and if I had looked into his identity theft problem yet.

Gordie went down to the café to get some coffee, and I stood in the shower, soaping my body and hair until I was washed clean of the smell of smoke, even if it was imaginary at that point. I put on some clean clothes from the suitcase I'd taken to Catalina and sat down at the small desk in our room while I wielded the hotel's blow dryer to dry my hair.

"Coffee," Gordie said, coming in with two cups in hand.

"Grateful, thanks." He put the coffee cup in front of me on the desk and leaned over to kiss the top of my head.

"I know you were reacting from the shock last night. It's OK if that's as far as you want to take it."

"I don't know Gordie, but I appreciate your company. Like, really appreciate it." He smiled and sat on the edge of the bed, coffee cup in his hand.

"All good, Mac. Let's just get you sorted, right?"

"I've had a call from the sheriff. I have to go over to their marina office and speak with them, call my boat insurance company, figure out where to stay, all that."

"I have a roomy long-stay suite in Culver City. You're welcome to stay there while I'm here for the next couple of weeks."

"Thanks for the offer, but I expect I can take a monthly lease on a studio in the marina where my boat was parked. I lived there before Peter."

"Peter?"

"My ex. Two years ex."

"Ah yes, grand. At least you have options."

"Yes, I have options."

Gordie went back to Culver City while I walked back to the dock to see what was left of Caerleon and take some photos of her remains for my insurance claim. Her superstructure above the water line was a tangled, black mess of melted fiberglass gel coat and metal. Her cockpit was buried under the mess, and there was no remaining cabin entrance, if anything of the interior of the boat had even survived. There was no way to get aboard her, let alone enter the cabin to retrieve any surviving items. There was police tape stretched across from the dock box on one side of the slip to a dock box on the other side, cordoning her off. There was a floating boom around her, a precautionary measure in the event of any leaking fuel. A few gawkers from the neighboring apartments and docks stopped to survey the sad remnants. I felt empty. Just another loss. Just stuff.

Instead of heading over to the sheriff station in the car, I walked over to the 400 dock, where my Chris-Craft runabout had been moved from her slip adjacent to Caerleon to get her out of harm's way after the fire started.

The Chris was just 20 feet long but packed a 270-horse Volvo engine, a small cuddy cabin, and two cushy captain's seats with a bench seat behind, and a teak swim step in the back. A Chris-Craft "heritage" version, she sported teak strips along her sides and at the helm. With a dark blue fiberglass hull outlined by sleek red racing stripes, she was a thing of beauty. She wasn't quite the all-mahogany vintage Chris-Crafts of my youth on New Hampshire lakes, but her fiberglass hull was more suited to salt water, not to mention less upkeep. I pulled the canvas cover off the helm, stored it in the dock box, and started her engine room blower. After a few minutes, I sat behind the wheel and turned the key. The inboard engine rumbled to life. I left the gears in neutral while I untied her dock lines, then gave a gentle push off the dock, reversed her out of the slip, then pointed her bow toward the main channel and the sheriff's station.

Halfway across the main channel, I changed my mind about arriving promptly for the 10 AM appointment. I kept the boat on the straightaway, then turned to starboard to follow the channel between the north and south jetties, toward the cross jetty that hosted the flagpole. From there, I turned north into Santa Monica Bay. Sea birds were lined up on the rocks along the jetty. Gulls, egrets, pelicans, diversities co-existing in a reasonable manner that frequently eluded human societies.

I'd been cruising at just 8 knots, the designated speed limit in the channel, until clearing the entrance to the north jetty. I pushed the throttle up until the boat got up on a plane at about 20 knots. The sea conditions in the bay weren't conducive to a fully open throttle, as the swells were topping about 3 to 4 feet. It wasn't a rough sea by any stretch for a larger boat, but they made my runabout dance and sway over the crests and troughs. The rush I felt as the waves buffeted the boat and the occasional spray that hit me in the face, was familiar and calming.

There were few other boats out. There wasn't enough wind to satisfy sailors at that time of day, but a couple of power boats were heading back in toward the marina, probably after an early appointment with fish. I counted myself lucky to have the Chris. She'd be a fine tender for the bigger boat I was imagining in my future to replace Caerleon. I circled to port after passing the Santa Monica Pier, then cruised back to the marina, taking the north entrance, then cutting her speed back and swinging into the far-right traffic lane, keeping the aid to navigation buoys, marking the no sail zone, on my port side.

I cut the speed down to 5 knots as I turned into the channel, then slowed her down to approach the dingy dock near Fisherman's Village and slung her fenders over the side. After tying her lines to the dock, I cut the engine and walked over to the sheriff's station. I was only 45 minutes late.

"Mackenzie Brody, here to see Sheriff Skinner about a boat fire," I said to the woman in uniform who was behind the reception desk. "He's expecting me." I knew a few of the sheriffs by sight and name, but Skinner was new to me and I to him.

"Brody" he said, without further introduction. "Let's go around to the back." I followed him around to what was obviously the evidence locker behind the station.

"I'm sorry, I have nothing to tell you except a witness saw someone jump off your boat just before the fire started. Whenever arson is suspected, the fire arson investigator gets involved and will do an inspection. Any prints, if there were any, would have been destroyed by the fire. No CCTV in the area. Meanwhile you can have your binocs back." He handed me a pair of binoculars off a shelf containing assorted recovered stolen merchandise. They were partially blackened and covered in soot.

"That's it? That's all they got off the boat?"

"Everything else was a total loss. These were found in the ruins of the cockpit, not the cabin. The cabin wasn't accessible – collapsed.".

"Yeah, I'd left them on the helm." The sheriff gave me a shrug of his broad shoulders.

"Who was the witness? What did they see?"

"I don't recall the name – it was someone who lives in the adjacent apartments and was walking their dog along beside the marina. They saw someone get out of the cockpit of your boat and head up the gangway. Appeared to be a male but they weren't close enough to see anything else. And they didn't connect it to the fire right away as it took a few minutes for the flames and smoke to start up."

"Who is the arson investigator?" I asked.

"Johnson is his name. Brad – with the LA County Fire Arson Investigation Section. He'll get in touch after he has looked around. You can give your insurance company his name and they'll do their own thing."

"Okay."

"Any idea who might have had it in for you?"

"Don't know. I'm a private investigator. But I haven't annoyed anyone lately that I can think of. I mostly look for missing people."

"Give it some thought. Boat torch jobs don't usually happen without some impetus. If it's not a domestic situation, there might be a bad actor in your life." I sighed and brushed some of the soot off my binoculars.

"How long before I can pull her out of the water? I'll have her towed to the yard to get hauled out as long as she stays afloat to get her there. I know she's headed to the salvage yard after that."

"After the arson guy does his inspection, you can have her moved. Your marina put a boom around her, but there appears to be no threat of an oil or diesel leak, so she can be towed to the yard. Slowly."

"Thanks," Sheriff Skinner saw me back to the entrance of the building. I walked along the shorefront by the dated Fisherman's Village storefronts and got back in my Chris. I was beginning to feel detached from my personal loss. I was recovering from the shock of having my house on the water burn down and my brain was ticking along into investigator mode as time passed. I didn't usually work on criminal investigations, but it was the same process used in 20 years of investigating civil cases and missing persons. Who, where, what, motive, and opportunity all began their quiet seduction of my gray matter. Bottom line. Some fuckhead torched my boat. Who and why?

CHAPTER SEVENTEEN

It was a strange feeling, motoring away from the Sheriff's station. I now had a 20-foot runabout, a car, a laptop, a few clothes, some expensive French moisturizing lotion that I'd bought on the way home from Ireland in Duty Free, my PI and driver's licenses, my American and Irish passports, credit cards, several pieces of furniture in storage, a pair of sooty binocs, and a business to run. I drove back to the marina and parked the car in my usual spot, then walked to the leasing office at the apartments adjacent to the marina, trailing my small rolling suitcase from the Catalina trip. They had one 600 square foot studio apartment available. I filled out the forms, wrote them a check for the deposit and first month's overpriced rent for a month-by-month arrangement, and walked over to the ground-floor unit. It wasn't exactly ground level; it was one flight up above the parking garage. I took stock of the apartment, then sat on the floor and called a guy who had helped me move once before, asking him to pick up what I had in storage and deliver it that day. At least I would have a bed to sleep in.

I met my mover and his helper at the storage facility on Sepulveda Boulevard and watched him load his truck with a queen bedframe and mattress, a small couch, a desk chair, a desk, two lamps, and a few boxes of kitchen supplies and dishes. After we'd wiped out the contents of the storage unit, I went to the office and signed off on closing it and followed the truck back to the marina. After they unloaded the boxes and furniture into the studio apartment, set up the bed and took their leave, I stood there looking around trying to think what to do next.

The apartment came equipped with air con, a re-frigerator, dishwasher, microwave, oven, bath and washer and dryer, but I didn't have one bed sheet or towel, so my next stop was a store, followed by a trip to some other store to replenish my wardrobe to a modest degree. Meanwhile I was on the phone with an internet provider to order a modem and get my Wi-Fi running. I felt like I was 18 and getting ready to live in a college dorm.

Gordie rang my cell as I was unloading my pur-chases into a cart in the garage to take up to the studio, and we agreed to meet at Beach & Brew near the Venice Pier for a drink and dinner.

"Just stuff, right," I said, over a glass of white Sonoma wine, homemade corn chips, and guacamole.

"Cheers to that," Gordie said, clinking my glass with his. We were sitting by the large open windows of the restaurant, with the traffic and inhabitants of Venice going by in a steady river. The street rattle and hum, rather than irritating, was a comforting whitewash.

"I'm exhausted. I have to get back to work on this case and Peter is waiting for me to look into his identity theft. And I have a million calls to make to sort out the charred ruins of my boat." Gordie set down his glass and smiled at me with his head slightly cocked to one side. It made me laugh. "I'm a wreck, Gordie!"

"You're not a wreck... well maybe a shipwreck." We both laughed. "What's next then, on the Rowan front?"

"I want to check out both Derek Baker and Jonathan Chambers. And also I want to have a look at Chambers Environmental's yard in LA."

"I have a shoot this week for the studio, but I'll be there if you need me."

I got back to my apartment to find my ex at the door. It was the same way he used to show up unannounced to the boat when he was in between flights from LAX.

"Peter! How did you know where to find me?"

"Your dockmaster. He seems to know everything. I got the full low down on the boat fire. What a mess. What the hell happened to Caerleon?"

"Well, I didn't leave the stove on, that's for sure. I was in Catalina overnight and came back to find her in flames." I opened the door and we walked into my spartan surroundings.

"Jesus, I'm so sorry Mac." He hugged me, which I accepted. After all, my home had just burned down. And she used to be his before the divorce. All six feet two inches of him felt comforting.

I filled Peter in on the particulars of the sheriff, fire department, and the insurance company procedures, as far as I understood them. "It's all in slow motion. She'll get hauled out this week and sent to the boat graveyard. She's not gonna sink in her slip before then, but she's a total loss, obviously."

"Caerleon's burned out hull is quite the tourist attraction in the meantime. There was a crowd at the railing. You could sell tickets!" Peter held me again when I started crying."

"When was the last time you ate?"

"Had some snacks. Fridge is empty."

"Let's go get something. At least to drink."

We walked over to the bar at the Marriottt Hotel and sat at the terrace bar overlooking the marina as the sun was setting, turning the sky a solid pink in a reflection of the sunset on the opposite side of the building.

"I'll start your identity theft research tomorrow, Peter, I promise. Have you heard any more from the powers that be into the hack of your identifiers?"

"Not a thing. Been in touch with the banks, made a fraud report to the feds. I have done everything I can – changed all my passwords, put freezes on all my credit accounts. The only new thing I've seen is that someone tried to get cell phone service in my name. I had a call from the company, and they shut it down."

"Did you get copies of all three credit company reports to see if anything slipped through before you put the freezes on?"

"Yes – nothing else has shown."

"I'll run my databases and see if any other strange things pop up. Sometimes you'll see a new address hit the databases if someone tried to get service or a subscription in your name before the freezes were put on the accounts."

"Thanks Mac. How's your other case going? Any luck in Catalina?"

"Not much. Still no body, so there's hope."

"You're the eternal optimist."

"I'm paid to be."

Peter and I finished eating, then he left to catch another plane. I walked back to my new temporary digs, unpacked, set up the new modem and got my Wi-Fi working, then sat down at the small desk with my laptop. I was determined to fight the fatigue I was feeling from the last two days.

Digging into every public database I could find for California's regulatory agencies, I came up with a number of citations issued to Chambers Environmental for violations of hazardous material transport regulations over the past 5 years. They were also sued by the Department of Toxic Substances Control the prior year for repeat violations and paid a hefty six figure fine to avoid getting shut down. A pattern of disregard for environmental regulations was obvious. Not that they were much different than a lot of waste management companies I'd run across investigating pollution cases. It could be a nasty business with a mix of shady operators. Not always, but often enough. Chambers fit right into the category of waste management haulers who were skirting the law as much as possible. I nearly fell asleep at the desk before crashing into the freshly made bed for the night.

CHAPTER EIGHTEEN

In the morning, while waiting on an interminable hold on the phone to speak with my boat insurance agent, I logged into one of my PI databases. I punched in Peter's name and DOB. I located the listing for him at his current address and then ran a more comprehensive report for whatever public records might hit the data base. The report came up with the two Compton addresses listed as 'former' addresses, that hit when I made a preliminary pass a few days earlier, where I knew he had never lived. There was an address in Denver where I knew Peter had never lived. There was another additional address that hadn't show up before. It was in Palm Desert; a couple of hours drive east out the Interstate 10. Peter's database report also listed Caerleon, since he'd previously owned and documented the vessel as required with the Coast Guard.

I did some research on the Palm Desert address, which showed a single-family home with a resident/

owner by the name of Robert Smith. When I tried to run a separate comprehensive report for Smith to turn up prior addresses, litigation, liens, criminal history, relatives, etc., the record was a jumble of inaccurate information, none of which seemed to pertain to a Robert Smith living at the Palm Desert address. Common names were an incredible nuisance to research. His online trail was a mess, complicated by the common name and mis-matched dates of birth. According to the jumbled online hits, he could be 57 or 29. There were also no current landline or mobile phone numbers for him in Palm Desert. Robert Smith was a ghost.

On a whim, I ran my own name in the public databases, and sure enough, Robert Smith's Palm Desert address also popped up in a recent hit in my address record, as did the Denver address with no name attached to it other than mine and Peter's. My name was alternately listed as Mackenzie Brody, Mackenzie Girard, or Mackenzie Smith, although I'd never taken Peter's last name and never had any association with anyone named Smith residing in Palm Desert, or anyone in Denver. My boat ownership, since Caerleon had a Certificate of Documentation with the US Coast Guard, was reported the same as in Peter's online record, although without the boat's marina location, only vessel name and description.

It wasn't unusual that my information had been mixed up with Peter's, since the online public records are often cross contaminated amongst relations, associates, or unrelated persons who shared the same address at some point, but it was clear that someone who had gained access to Peter's identity likely had access to mine as well. And anyone looking to find Caerleon, whether they thought Peter or I were current owners, could extrapolate the boat's location by calling around local marinas and asking if Caerleon was berthed there. This opened up the possibility that Caerleon's torching could have been related to either of us.

Peter's identity details had likely been shared on the web, possibly for purchase, as hacked or stolen IDs frequently are, so any number of people could have picked up on it. Someone with a beef with Peter or me could have lit a match to Caerleon in retribution. On the other hand, if anyone was looking to find and aggravate me connected with any of my past or current cases, they wouldn't have too much trouble finding their mark.

Between the current investigation for a missing Irishwoman and looking into Peter's identify theft, I didn't have time to sit around and mull over the loss of Caerleon. It was depressing, at any rate, to hang out in my expensive marina bed-sit with three pieces of furniture. I shut down my laptop, grabbed my purse, and went down to the car. I drove out of the marina and picked up the 405 South to Long Beach for a quick check of Chambers Environmental's yard, then I was going to pick up the 10 freeway going east for the two-hour drive to Palm Desert. I wanted to knock on Robert Smith's door and see if the ghost was home, and what, if anything, he had to do with stealing Peter's identity.

CHAPTER NINETEEN

Torn fragments of clouds move
across an unsettled sky
like hieroglyphics
over an unsettled city,
giving ethereal instructions
for those who wait,
lined up along the boulevard,
waiting for a miracle.

The Chambers Environmental equipment yard in Long Beach was surrounded by a five-foot-tall fence. It covered about a half-acre in a neighborhood dominated by industrial buildings, many of which were probably tied to the harbor operations, in that it was not much more than a mile from LA-Long Beach Port and the container shipyards. The entrance gate was propped open and a pockmarked asphalt road lead from the entrance to a dirt yard with several low buildings and a couple of derelict trailers. Viewed from the street, I could see several trucks and a host of 55-gallon drums, some of which were metal and others plastic, positioned in groups alongside two of the structures.

As is typical for Southern California, spring weather hadn't produced much rain, and the sand and gravel surface was dry. I parked my car on the street out in front of the gate, and as I was approaching the gate on foot, a truck drove out, stirring up a cloud of dust in its wake.

Once just inside the gate, I didn't see any humans, but a pack of dogs came out from somewhere and were running across the yard in my direction, barking up a ferocious storm. There were at least three of them, a couple of pit bulls and one mix of something. I stopped in my tracks, aware that I had nowhere to go and couldn't outrun the dogs. Just as they were within about 20 yards, I heard a loud whistle followed by a yell, and the dogs turned around and ran back toward the building, stirring up more dust. The animal wrangler walked toward me after ushering the dogs into the door of one of the buildings. He looked about 40, sagging pants overseen by a large stomach, soiled sweatshirt, and a dirty baseball cap to match.

"Who you lookin' for, lady?" He met my eyes, then looked at the notebook I had in one hand. He probably thought I was selling insurance or something. I didn't offer an explanation.

"The owner if he's here - Mr. Chambers," I said, holding my ground.

"He ain't here but should be back soon. If you want to wait for him, take a seat in the trailer." He pointed toward the smaller of the two trailers. The trailer's tongue was resting on a couple of cinder blocks and the side window was boarded up with a piece of plywood. The metal around the door was rusted. The door stood open.

I stepped up into the interior of the trailer, which was lit by a small lamp on a rectangular table. The structure creaked slightly under my weight. There were two wooden chairs at the table. I pulled one out, brushed off the dusty seat and sat down. I kept my hands off the surface of the stained Formica table and looked around the trailer in the dim light. Aside from the table, there was a built-in Naugahyde couch along the side that was partially covered by a blanket. The couch back showed several tears, with the stuffing coming out. The overall smell in the trailer was of dog. Patches of dog hair on the floor evidenced that the trailer had been used as a kennel at some point in time. The clumps of short hair were mixed with what looked like rat pellets. I wasn't so concerned by the dust and dog hair, but the prospect of a rat running across the table in front of me made me shudder.

I waited 15 minutes, which I spent regretting my foolishness in attempting to interview the senior Chambers, before a heavy-set bald man approached and stepped into the trailer.

He pulled up the other chair closest to the door and sat down, the chair creaking under his weight. He put his hands down on the table in front of his truly substantial stomach. "Who are you?"

"Mackenzie Brody. I'm looking into the disappearance of a young Irish woman, Rowan Collins, for her father. I think you met her briefly, according to your son."

"Jonathan said you were a pain in the ass. You also harassed my son in Catalina at the yard, so I'm told." Chambers wiped his hand across his unkempt beard, catching what was probably remnants of his lunch.

"There was no harassment, let's be clear about that Mr. Chambers. I've spoken with several people, looking for some clue as to what could have happened. A woman has disappeared and is possibly dead. There are a lot of questions to ask."

"Don't expect any help from us. You're not a cop. We don't have to talk to you. You're on your own, lady, and you'd be smart to watch your step."

I didn't sense any way to soften him up and gain his cooperation. I figured I'd be lucky to get out of the yard without the dogs being set loose. "Well, thanks anyways," I said, getting out of the chair. The only problem was that he was blocking the exit. He stood up at the same time I did and filled the door frame. After a moment of tense silence, the two of us staring at each other, he stepped aside.

"You've got thirty seconds to get off my yard before the pits come out."

"I'll be on my way then." I stepped gingerly through the rusted metal door frame and into the yard. I walked without looking back. I heard barking as I pulled open the now closed gate and closed it behind me. "Fucker," I said to no one in particular, as I got into the car.

I don't know what I'd expected of Chambers, but I certainly didn't get offered a cup of tea along with any information about his meeting with Rowan, or any insight as to his relationship with Jonathan. He was threatening and a bully. I'd have to work around him if I wanted to get any further with his son.

The drive to Palm Desert in the middle of the day avoided most of the traffic from residents who commuted to LA for work and back at rush hour. I drove by the wind turbine forest between the canyons near Palm Springs, where the blades were spinning casually. I kept trying to find some synchronicity from one machine to the other as I drove past them, but there was a randomness to their movement, like an out-of-rhythm orchestra in need of a conductor. The hills of the San Bernardino National Forest on the other side of the 10 freeway were still green from an earlier dose of winter rain. The desert looked inviting and as close to lush as it would get before the summer sun burnt it to brown.

Robert Smith's house was in a residential community in Palm Desert. Once I exited the freeway at Monterey Avenue, I crossed Dinah Shore Drive, Gerald Ford Drive, and Frank Sinatra Drive before picking up the Pines to Palms Highway. I wondered if you got a street named after you in Palm Desert when the major thoroughfares in Palm Springs were already taken by Bob Hope and Sonny Bono.

I drove around in the quiet neighborhood with appropriately western theme named trails referencing a broken arrow, a silver spur, and a buckboard. The houses were predominately 1950s era low rises consisting of one story with a pool. White's house was the same, with the addition of a large driveway beside it that held an RV almost the same size as the house. In addition to the whale of a recreational vehicle, there was a Tesla in the driveway. It was not plugged in, leading me to believe the owner might be home in between errands.

A late 50s something Caucasian man answered the door in a golf shirt and shorts, with an iced drink in his hand. Probably fresh off 18 holes. "Robert White?" I asked.

"Hi there, what's up?" he said, pleasant enough, as if he expected I was there to refund an overpayment of his golf club dues.

I had immediate regrets of imagining I'd find a scheming con artist armed with a host of phishing scams and a .9 mil, which would have made complete sense. This didn't look promising.

"I'm not sure I have the right house. I'm a private investigator, looking into some identify theft for a client. The web records listed your name attached to this address, maybe related to a recent attempt to get a loan in my client's name."

"Wow, that's interesting. Come in and let's have a chat. Your name is…?"

"Mackenzie Brody. Thanks, maybe we can figure out what was going on and see if someone was impersonating you online." Robert White gently blocked a rather large tabby cat with his foot to keep the cat from making a hasty escape out the front door while I entered. The cat did an about-face and wandered off into another room.

Robert White's residence was sparkling and ultra-modern. He signaled me to a chair at a glass kitchen table and put down his drink. "Can I get you something? Soda? Water?"

"No thanks, I'm good but I appreciate you asking." He pulled up his chair and sat opposite me. He smelled like Dr. Bronner's peppermint soap. Squeaky clean like his kitchen.

"Do you mind terribly showing me some identification, Mackenzie?" I pulled out my wallet from my purse and showed him my California PI license ID.

"Thanks," he said, after giving it a brief look.

"I have access to a subscription database as an investigator – it's all stuff from the public record, but it's useful when I need to go looking for people or do a background investigation. My client had his identity stolen and asked me to look into the online record and see if anything turned up. I came across your name and this address, mixed in with his information. I just wondered if someone had recently tried to use your identity to try and get credit or a loan, anything like that?"

Robert White looked at me, then at his drink while he tapped on the table with the long fingers of his right hand. "I did have an issue with a credit card recently. Not sure that might be related. There was a mysterious charge, and I had to cancel it and get a new card."

"Do you mind if I ask what type of business you're in?"

"Software and AI programming. I have my own company, Digital Express."

"Huh. Do you have an LA office?"

"Yeah, we have a small office on the Westside in Santa Monica, but most of us work remotely."

"Any chance you have a guy who works for you or subcontracts named Derek Baker?"

"Don't know that name. We only have two dozen employees. I would know him."

"Hang on just a minute," I said, pulling out my phone. Here's a photo of Baker – look familiar?"

"Ah yes, that's Peter Girard. We brought him on recently to do some remote programming. We on-boarded him at the Santa Monica office, he did some assignments remotely, then he quit." This was getting more fun by the minute.

"Well, that's interesting Robert. His name isn't Peter Girard. That's the name of my client who had his identity stolen. This guy is Derek Baker."

White looked at me with his mouth open. "How can that be? I had our HR person check his credentials of course. He seemed to be a decent programmer."

"Do you remember the date when you met him here and hired him?"

"Approximate because it was at the start of a new contract - would have been just last month."

"I can't guess why he would have used Peter's name. I will let my client know. Do you know if Baker is in LA currently?"

"He was in town recently - he came into the Santa Monica office last week to say he was taking another job offer."

"Do you know what day that was?"

"Not sure but it was just a few days ago. I wasn't there but got an email from my HR."

"Was he claiming to be a US citizen?"

"Well, yes, we knew he was Irish, but he had a California driver's license, and a social security number along with a local address. He'd said he was a dual citizen, and that he had family in the States and in Ireland. Part of the brief time he was working for us he was working remotely from Dublin."

"Do you think you could provide me with whatever local address he gave you?"

"Yes, I can get it from the office and send it to you. Is email okay?"

"Sure, here's a card with my contact info. I appreciate it."

"I hope your client didn't get ripped off. I'll let our HR know and confirm he has absolutely no access to our systems – which we do anyways whenever there is a change in personnel. He could have had an intention to steal clients from us. But as far as I know, he didn't. I appreciate you letting me know, Mackenzie."

I left Robert White's house more mystified than ever, wondering what Derek Baker was up to and why he'd chosen Peter to steal an ID. I had a growing suspicion that I had led him to Peter, and that he had then targeted Peter to get to me. I had no clue what this all had to do with Rowan Collins, or possibly my boat being torched.

CHAPTER TWENTY

The drive back from Palm Desert was fast, all things considered, as I was going against the rush hour traffic. While on the road, I called Peter and gave him the rundown on Derek Baker using his identity. Since Peter had already frozen his credit accounts and changed passwords on his cards, there wasn't much else he could do except keep any eye out for unusual activity with his bank or other finances. I arrived back in the marina close to dinnertime. I rang Gordie and he picked up right away.

"Hi there, what's up Mac?"

"Fancy dinner in Redondo Beach? I want to have another look at Jonathan's boat, preferably while he's not there."

"Sure. We can go to Redondo in my rental if you want. I'll be done here in about a half hour."

"Text me when you're close and I'll meet you out front of my apartment building. And bring your camera."

The drive to the south bay took a while in rush hour traffic. At least I wasn't driving.

"How was it at Chambers' yard?"

"Good considering the pit bulls didn't get to me, and old man Chambers just bluffed and bullied, with no particular follow-through."

"Pit bulls?"

"Badly treated ones, and/or trained to go for blood. Security system of choice in some neighborhoods."

"Christ!"

"Even more interesting was my visit to the home of Robert Smith in Palm Desert. His name and address came up very recently on Peter's database and mine."

"What does that mean?"

"Could be a few things, but for sure someone was using Peter's identifiers to get up to no good, and it was related to Robert Smith with the desert address. The kicker is that Smith's computer firm had recently hired Derek Baker to do some programming under the pseudonym of Peter Girard."

"What the?" Gordie didn't finish his sentence as he nearly swerved the car into the next lane, then corrected.

"I don't know his motive, but it's starting to look like Baker is trying to get me off this case. He could have mined Peter's ID info and my own off the web, since it was likely getting circulated among the 'hacks for purchase' websites. And it looks like he was in town both when Rowan disappeared, which we knew from the Catalina trip when the shore boat captain recognized his photo, and now this week, coinciding with my boat's demise."

"Maybe he traced you to Caerleon and decided to make a point with some accelerant."

"That's what I'm wondering, but it's conjecture. I can't see any way to prove that unless the arson investigator from the fire department comes up with some physical evidence to link him to the fire. No one at my marina recalls seeing someone near my boat, and there are no cameras there. The cyber trail on the identity theft would be a maze, so probably no help."

"He could be trying to get you off the trail because he doesn't like what you're doing. I don't know, maybe he's obsessed or wacko."

"And Jonathan could be telling the truth. Just a prick. Him and the entire male side of his waste disposal family. I'd venture a guess they have some things to hide from a close look at their environmental compliance record, but whether it involves Rowan or not…"

"What do you want to do?"

"I want to stay on track with Jonathan. I still don't like the looks of him. I know he's lying to me."

"What are you looking for on his boat?"

"Blood."

It was dark by the time we pulled into the marina in Redondo Beach. It had been a long day and a lot of travel for me already, but I was on my second wind.

"Why exactly aren't we leaving this to the sheriff, Mac?" Gordie asked as we valet parked at the restaurant beside the docks and got out to walk over toward Jonathan's boat slip.

"They've already ruled Jonathan out as a person of interest. We need something to make him look interesting again to them."

"Alright, whatever you think."

"Where's your camera?"

"In my pocket. I brought my compact one with a good lens for close-ups. Probably more appropriate for this job and less obvious."

"Great." We went through the locked gate down the ramp towards his boat when another boater was coming out. They didn't give us a second look. I couldn't see anyone else visible on the dock or on neighboring boats who might get curious as to our presence, and I didn't see any CCTV cameras secured to the closest building by the gate, which held the boater bathrooms.

There were still two 55-gallon metal drums sitting in the cockpit. The hatch to the cabin was closed and had a padlock on it. "Not much to see," Gordie said.

"Can you take a pic of those drums, and the floor of the cockpit where those black marks are?" Gordie hopped on board and took the shots. The obvious narrow black tread marks on the floor of the cockpit looked like they came from using a dolly, and the gel coat flooring was scuffed up as though he repeatedly moved some heavy objects around on it.

"I don't see any markings on the drums. Just rust. Are those tops secured in any way, Gordie?" He reached over and nudged the top of the drum closest to him, then the other. They were both on tight. He stood there for a moment, curiously studying the boat.

"What?" He wiped his hand on his pants.

"Got any equipment to detect blood?" he asked, kneeling to take some close-ups of the gel coat flooring.

"Nope, sorry."

"Does your expertise include forensic science?"

"Nope. But I've seen twelve seasons of 'Bones' and twenty-six seasons of 'Silent Witness', so that should qualify me for something." Gordie chuckled as he stood up.

"Those drums are – what – about 50 pounds empty? Let alone full of anything." Gordie knocked on the sides of both drums, which responded with hollow rings, and then he tried to tilt them up to one side, one at a time. They each moved to the pressure of his hand. "Empties," he added. "I wonder why metal drums instead of the plastic ones that are easier to move."

Gordie lifted a leg over the gunnel and back onto the dock. He stood there studying the boat. "Not easy to get these on and off, especially full."

"He could roll them out with a dolly onto the dock through this," I said, indicating the hinged part of the gunnel that could swing open. He'd have to put down a portable ramp to bridge the gap between the boat and dock. Maybe stored it in here?" I said, motioning to the dock box. It also had a padlock on it.

"Okay, let's get out of here," I said.

We sauntered up the dock like we belonged there, went through the gate, and walked around to the restaurant entrance. We went into the bar that overlooks the docks and ordered some drinks and a late dinner. "What else can I do to assist you in this endeavor?" Gordie asked, raising his beer glass. "Need any breaking and entering instead of just entering?"

"We need some surveillance of Jonathan, and to find out what's going on with Derek Baker. How much longer are you here?"

"A few weeks on the job probably, unless there are some production hold ups." He took my hand across the table. "Do you want another?" he said, indicating my empty wine glass.

"I'm good, thanks. I want to stay awake on the ride back. I have a colleague I can tap to get some eyes on Jonathan. My least favorite thing is to do surveillance. At least one of my least favorite things."

"What are the others?"

"Um..." "There must be more?" he said.

"Permanently losing people. As in they die. Top of the list."

"I get that."

"Rowan isn't in that category, Gordie. I've not given up on her."

"Neither have I. She's not... gone," he said, pausing strangely. I looked at him and he looked away, then shrugged, as we pushed our chairs back to leave, then headed back to the parking lot.

CHAPTER TWENTY-ONE

Gordie didn't stay over when he dropped me off at my apartment. He half asked, and I half declined, being still somewhat conflicted about an intimate relationship with him. I was also tired. Before I took the elevator up to my floor, I walked over to my boat and stood on the dock at her stern looking at the charred hull and tangled mess of black plastic wrapped in yellow police 'do not cross' tape.

"That's a sad sight," the marina's night security guard said, from his position on the railing above. "When is she getting hauled out?"

"I'll find out from the sheriff tomorrow. Soon to the boneyard. No doubt they'll send me a rather large bill for disposing of her."

"Good luck. I hope your boat insurance will cover it," he said.

"Yeah, me too." I went back up the ramp to the promenade and then walked over to my building. I wasn't looking forward to the sparsely furnished studio, but it had a comfortable queen bed, and I was ready for it.

In the morning I was on the phone first thing to the LA County Marina Sheriff's department. The first in a series of calls. Having your boat burn down generated almost as much red tape as losing your house in a wildfire.

Reception put me on hold until Sheriff Skinner picked up the call three minutes later. "The fire department have given their OK to have her towed over to the yard for haul-out. There are no fuel leaks, so no environmental concerns with moving her. Have your insurance company do the inspection after they've pulled her up on the hard."

"Has the arson investigator had a look at her yet?"

"He did yesterday. The fire was intentional - likely started in the cabin, after someone broke the lock on the cabin door. No luck recovering fingerprints due to the fire."

"Have there been any similar boat fires in the marina lately? Wondering if this could be a one off or more."

"We haven't responded to a boat fire in this marina in six months. No indication of a serial pyro at work."

"Okay thanks. I'll contact the yard and have Sea Tow pull her over there as soon as they have room to haul her out."

After calls to the insurance company, boat yard and Sea Tow, I had Caerleon lined up to be towed from the dock on her last sad journey across the main channel to the boatyard for her haul-out and insurance inspection.

Next up was meeting with the colleague I leaned on to do surveillance when it was needed for a case. Barry Silva was an experienced local boater and a good friend. Post-divorce, I'd initially hoped he would ask me out, until he told me he was gay.

Barry set up a solo PI business after he'd had enough of the legal profession, and he was having much more fun doing surveillance and other types of investigative field work. He also had a van with several different magnetic signs for its sides, indicating on any particular day that he was either a plumber, an electrician, or a computer repairman. His presence for some hours parked on the street would not arouse curious neighbors.

In any case, as a licensed investigator, Barry knew from experience that if a cop was called by a nosey neighbor to check you out on a stationary surveillance, identifying yourself as a PI on a surveillance would help. If you flashed your ID when they came to the window of your vehicle, they would usually leave you alone. We sometimes gave a heads-up to the local police station watch stander to let them know we'd be parked somewhere; in case a neighbor called the station to report a stalker.

I got to the lobby of the Marriottt ten minutes ahead of lunch, and Barry was already there. He sported a well-worn baseball cap, as per usual. The rest of him looked like any other 50-something sailor in the lobby bar, wearing a weather-ready Helly Hanson jacket, jeans, and scuffed up boat shoes. He lived on a shiny forty-five foot Canadian-built power yacht over on A basin by the gas dock. His liveaboard was not shabby by any means.

"What new adventure have you got for me, Mac?"

"A very lovely few days traversing from Venice to Redondo Beach to Long Beach, with a possible side trip to Catalina."

"Sounds like the dream assignment."

"Here's your man," I said, showing him a photo on my phone. "Jonathan Chambers, thirty-year-old James Dean look-alike, who keeps an old Bertram sport fisher in Redondo named Flight Risk."

"You can tell a lot by what people name their boats."

"You're right about that. Jonathan apparently illegally hauls drums from Catalina to his family's waste disposal yard in Long Beach called Chamber's Waste Disposal, or maybe hauls them somewhere else."

"Like?"

"Don't know. The sea, possibly? I would venture a guess that it's not going to a licensed landfill. I'd like to catch him in the act of whatever. He said he picks up stuff like waste oil from the island occasionally and brings it back to their yard in Long Beach."

"Huh. And why do you want to track this handsome white boy? Aside from his environmental crimes."

"He was dating the Irish woman, Rowan Collins, whom I've been tasked with finding, when she went missing from a Catalina outing with him in February."

"Ah. No body?"

"Right, no body."

"What do our esteemed law enforcement colleagues think of Jonathan? Is he a suspect in her disappearance?"

"No, they've passed on him. I'm not so sure though. One of the shore boat staff in Avalon saw him get into a dingy the night of her disappearance with a woman, though couldn't say if it was Rowan or not. And Jonathan has been rather touchy with me, as has his brother at the Catalina yard, and his father at the Long Beach yard."

"You've managed to irritate the entire family already? That's so like you, Mac," he said, smiling.

"This won't be like the Pasadena surveillance, Barry. I promise."

"You mean I won't have two Rottweilers and a large angry man chasing me back to my van if I get out to have a look around?"

"Well, just don't go into the Long Beach yard. There are guard dogs there. I've already been introduced."

I filled Barry in on the address details, Jonathan's car and boat information, and asked the server for our bill.

"How's Caerleon?"

"Oh Barry, I was hoping you wouldn't ask." He looked at me with raised eyebrows.

"She was torched a few days ago. I came home from Catalina to find the good ole' 110 and 310 fireboats hosing her down."

"Oh man. That was the other night? I heard the sirens from over on my boat. Hadn't heard what the occasion was though. Anything to do with this Mr. Chambers?"

"I don't know. There's another guy kicking around town who may have it in for me. He'll be next on your list for keeping an eye on, if I can find out where he's staying."

"Where are you staying?"

"At the apartment complex beside my marina. Leased a studio there for the time being. Caerleon is getting hauled out over to the yard tomorrow. She's a total loss."

"That really sucks, Mac. I'm so sorry. Will you get another boat with the insurance settlement?"

"I don't know yet. My next boat might have sails though – as much as I loved Caerleon, there's the price of fuel and the environment to think about, even if a sailboat isn't as roomy to live on as a power boat."

"You'd do fine. Just get a big enough one."

"You know as well as I do that it's not just the cost of the ship. The slip fee with that live-aboard premium tacked on for a fifty-footer might not be in the budget. I'm not independently wealthy like you." He laughed.

"I was well off, until I got a boat. You take care, Mac. I'll get on Jonathan tomorrow – will try to catch him up heading out from his place in Venice in the AM and see what his day consists of. I may just take a guest slip at his marina with my boat - in case he heads out on his boat I can follow him."

"Don't get into any boat chases. I know yours is probably faster and you could catch him, but we just want to know what he's doing, not stop him from doing it. Unless of course we know it involves Rowan."

"I'll keep that in mind."

CHAPTER TWENTY-TWO

I went back to my apartment and checked my email. I had one from Robert Smith giving me the address of Derek Baker – it was the Dublin address I had already visited. Smith's note said that Baker, whom they knew as Peter Girard, hadn't given them an LA address as he said he was just temporarily staying with friends here. The information got me exactly nowhere.

Baker was in the wind if he was even still in the country. I had no location for him, and nothing solid to share with the cops that might tie him to Rowan or my boat fire. Maybe Gordie was right, he was just a whack job and small-time criminal obsessed with Rowan, or maybe obsessed with me because he knew I was looking for her and wanted to discourage me from pursuing the case or him. I had no idea why he might want to prevent me from doing so unless he had some culpability in her disappearance. Or Cara was right, and he was just scared of the attention from an investigator who could potentially uncover his cybercrimes.

On a whim, I decided to follow down another possible lead that had turned up in the research of Peter's ID theft. I sat at my laptop and punched in the Denver address I'd found hitting the databases for both of our names, to see what would turn up. I was thinking Peter might have gotten a post office box there, since his flights take him through Denver airport frequently and he often has an overnight in a Denver hotel before taking the helm of another plane the next day.

I ran the Denver address through one of my databases to see what type of property it was and what names were associated with it. It was listed as a single-family residence, and was the primary residence for someone named Angela Dunbar, 32 years old. She was sole owner as recently as the last year and for 10 years prior to that. The name didn't ring any bells with me. I had no idea how she might have turned up on our reports.

I plugged her name and address into a phone search and came up with three possible numbers for her name and address – all of which looked like mobile phone numbers rather than land lines. It would be the usual case of trying them all to see if any were current. I wasn't sure what I could accomplish by reaching her, but maybe her identity had been hacked as well, and it might be useful to talk to her. Since I like to have some idea who I'm reaching, I ran an employment search. Low and behold, she worked for an airline.

The first two numbers I dialed for Angela Dunbar were disconnected. The third number rang three times and was answered by an individual who sounded like an adolescent boy whose voice hadn't fully lowered yet.

"Hi, I'm calling for Angela. Is she home?" I said, trying to sound like her best long-lost friend.

"Who's this?" he said.

Before I could answer, I heard another voice telling him to give her the phone.

"I'm sorry, this is Angela's sister. Can I ask who you are? Were you a friend?"

The past tense didn't sound good. I hated this part, when you call trying to locate someone and find out they are no longer among the living, and the family is dealing with fresh grief. It has happened too often in my career.

"Yes, I mean no, I'm not a friend. My name is Mackenzie Brody. I'm sorry, this is awkward. Has something happened to her? I can explain why I was trying to contact her."

"Angela passed away two months ago. I'm her sister. I'm staying with her son, Jared. How can I help you?"

"You're very kind to take my call. I'm so sorry for the loss of your sister."

"What can I do for you?"

"I'm a private investigator in California, and I'm helping a man named Peter Girard sort out an identity theft that happened to him recently. I ran across Angela's name and address mixed up with Peter's personal identifying information in the public record, and wondered if she had a similar problem. Possibly she experienced someone using her identity or hacking her financial information."

"That I can explain. Perhaps Peter didn't tell you. He is Jared's father."

The phone nearly dropped out of my hand. I tightened my grip.

"I'm sorry, not sure I understand. Peter is my ex-husband. He had no prior marriage and never had any kids."

"This is awkward. Miss Mackenzie, Angela was taken ill very quickly with an aggressive cancer. I'm her only close family member and I came to take care of her in her last few months. She confided to me that a man named Peter Girard was Jared's father. She never told Peter she'd gotten pregnant, and she hadn't let Jared know who his father was. Before she died, she told them both."

I didn't know what to say. I just swallowed.

"Jared is six years old. Angela got ahold of Peter through a mutual friend of theirs before she passed, told him he had a son, and that Jared needed him."

"How long ago was that, if you know?"

"She died two months ago, so it would have been a couple of weeks before that. I know she felt some relief, knowing Jared would get to know his father."

"Had Peter been paying child support?"

"Not in the past, since Angela hadn't revealed to him that he had a son. She didn't put his name on the birth certificate. She didn't want to involve him, since their relationship had been so brief, and she wanted to raise Jared herself."

"Has Peter met Jared?"

"Not yet, but they plan to get together soon. We thought it best to give Jared a little time to grieve his mother before introducing Peter into his life."

"I see," I said, still at a loss for what to say.

"You're his stepmother, in whatever way that works with these splintered families. He will need a mother figure. I live here in Denver, so I can take care of him for now until his living arrangements are sorted out. I hope Peter will step in. We'll need to have that discussion. I'm not in a position to adopt Jared as I'm a single woman."

I felt like someone had just bashed me in the head, with the confusion from a concussion taking hold of my brain.

"Are you still there?" She said, after a long silent pause on my end.

"I'm sorry, I'll have to speak with Peter."

"I understand how difficult this must seem. Please take my name and personal cell phone number if you'd like to contact me. My name is Suzanne Dunbar." She read off her cell number, and I wrote it down.

"Thanks, I'll be speaking with Peter very soon."

"Jared's a great boy. You'll love him," she said, and hung up.

CHAPTER TWENTY-THREE

Like the undulating waves
or the flight of sea birds,
we ebb and surge,
reaching for strength,
until the heart finally seizes
the transition,
and grants that peace can co-exist
with the tides,
with the changes.

As I often did when I was faced with seemingly inscrutable circumstances, I turned off the computer and went down to my car, drove through Santa Monica on Ocean Boulevard, then north on Pacific Coast Highway up to Malibu. I parked in the beach lot just north of Point Dume and walked over to the base of the hill and up the path along the cliffs.

The wind had increased. It was kicking up white caps on the surface of the ocean, so the wind was blowing at least 7 to 10 knots. I took off my baseball cap before it blew away, and let the wind make a mess of my locks. I climbed up to a lookout point over the water along the cliff and leaned up against the fence. I saw what looked like a crest of a huge wave far off the coast, gradually coming towards shore. It was taking a southerly path and as it got closer, I could see that it was not a tsunami. It was a very large pod of dolphins. There must have been a couple hundred of them, swimming and leaping out of the water. As the dolphins kept going south along the coast and eventually disappeared from my view, I walked back down the path to the car. I was dreading the call to Peter, but it had to be done. I sat in my car in the parking lot at Point Dume and dialed him on my cell.

"Peter, we need to talk," I said, reaching him as he was in a cab on his way home from LAX.

"Sure, Mac, I'm almost home."

"I mean we need to talk now."

"Hang on, just getting out of the cab." I could hear him talking to the driver, and then the thump of his luggage hitting the ground. I waited until he had gotten into his condo and got back on the line.

"What's up, Mac?"

"I think you know, Peter. You have a son. You've had a son for six years. That's two years before the affair you admitted to that ended our marriage."

"Christ, Mac. How did you hear? I just found out a few weeks ago and was going to tell you."

If there's any truth to the description that one's blood is boiling, I could attest to its accuracy. I couldn't get out any more words, or more specifically no more than two words.

"Fuck you."

"I'm sorry, Mac."

"It was over two months ago that you found out and you didn't tell me. Not only does this indicate that you were having affairs well before you admitted to it, but the boy's aunt thinks I should now be his surrogate mother."

"Can we get together – how about tomorrow? Let's talk about it then."

"You lying piece of shit, Peter." The words were beginning to come faster.

"I have a son, Mac. I'm flabbergasted. I'm stunned. I don't know what to think."

"Well, good luck figuring out how it happened. Bastard." I hung up.

Whatever Peter was going to do about being a father, he was going to have to deal. I was not going to offer congratulations, or help, or step into a motherly role for the issue of my ex-husband's dalliance. I had to park that problem in another compartment in my head and see to my toasted boat. I started my car, drove out of the parking lot, and turned to starboard on PCH for the drive back to Marina del Rey.

On the way home I had a call from the towing company to arrange moving Caerleon over to the boat yard. The tow company had a boat available, and we agreed to meet as soon as I got back to the marina. I was glad for the distraction from the latest upheaval in my personal life.

After parking at my apartment, I walked over to Caerleon's dock and met the Sea Tow vessel. I untied Caerleon's lines from the cleats on both sides and slowly, manually, pushed her blackened form back out of the slip, while the tow boat driver grabbed her lines and secured her for a side tow. After they had the tow under control, I went to my car and drove to the yard to meet her there. The yard staff were ready for her and organized the heavy straps under her hull for the crane to lift her. She came out of the water like a dead whale. The crane slowly moved her onto the yard and into cradles that were prepositioned for her. The insurance inspector was already there and waiting.

"Charles Jenson," he said, putting out his hand for me to shake. With his other hand, he was holding a clipboard full of paper.

"Mackenzie Brody. I see you're not digital yet." I said, motioning to his clipboard, having expected him to be talking into a phone or tablet with his observations, and videoing the inspection process.

"My camera is in the car. I'm a bit new school and a bit old school. Been at this for a long time." Jenson was probably in his sixties. That gave me some reassurance at least, knowing he'd been doing this for a while.

"You've got the police report, I assume?"

"Yes, and the fire department report. Judged to be deliberately set, with no known culprit."

"That about sums it up, I'm afraid."

"They were able to count you out as having had a direct hand in it for the insurance proceeds, as your alibi for being en route back from Catalina checked out."

"I wouldn't have sabotaged my own home, Mr. Jenson."

"Caerleon is a beauty. Or was," he said.

"I'll leave you to it. I can't bear to look at her. I'm sure you guys will get back to me with whatever report you produce."

"We should have something to you by the end of next week. Barring any questions, we'll process the claim under your insurance, and the cost of her haul out and disposal should be covered as part of that."

"Thanks." I walked over to the parking lot without looking back.

CHAPTER TWENTY-FOUR

Barry called my cell while I was walking to my apartment from the garage. "How would you like a boat ride, Mac? Maybe first thing tomorrow?"

"What's up Barry? How's it going?"

"There's been some action with this guy right away. I moved my boat down to Redondo into a guest slip at his marina, so I'm in position if your man takes off somewhere and I can tail him. My berth is just a couple docks over, so I can see what's going on at his boat."

"That's convenient."

"First thing I noticed was that there were no drums in the cockpit – I know you'd seen two there yesterday. Then while I was there, your man shows up in a pick-up truck, and unloads a metal 55-gallon drum off the truck and down to his boat on a dolly. He transferred it onto his boat with a metal ramp that he'd had on the truck, then went back to the parking lot and took off in his truck. I got in my car and picked him up on the road – he went back to Venice to his apartment after that. I'm just thinking there's a good chance he might be taking that drum for a ride somewhere tomorrow."

"Maybe to pick up some waste in Catalina, or to drop some off somewhere?"

"That drum had to be full of something. He really struggled with the weight of it."

"Can you get on him early and if he heads to Redondo instead of the yard in Long Beach, give me a heads up and I'll meet you on your boat."

"That's a plan, Mac."

"I'll be ready to go early if it looks like he's heading for the island."

I spent the remainder of the evening at a restaurant that was within walking distance from my apartment, having dinner and a couple of glasses of wine. Like most of the other patrons who were eating solo, I spent dinner staring at my phone, thinking about what I'd said to Peter, regretting my reaction, and trying to decide whether to call him. In the end, I didn't do it. I walked back to my apartment and got into bed with my tablet to stream an episode of a British cop show. It wasn't one of the especially good ones, of which there are many, but it satisfied my need for mindless entertainment.

The phone call came in from Barry at 6:30 AM. "He's on the move and looks to be heading for the boat. Come on down if you want to join me."

"On my way," I said, pulling on clothes as I spoke.

Barry had his boat engine running when I arrived. He backed out of the slip as soon as I hopped on board, eased the boat away from the slip and into the main channel.

"Jonathan is ahead of us by just a few minutes. We should be able to catch him outside the harbor."

The speed limit in the marina is 5 knots, so as to not rock boats with wake while they are in their slips. I went up on the deck as we coasted through the marina and pulled in the fenders on the starboard and port sides, laying them along the walkways beside the cabin. When we got near the entrance to Redondo Beach Harbor, Jonathan's boat was just exiting past the breakwater and ramping up speed. We were able to follow suit a few minutes behind and keep him in sight.

There were a few early morning fishermen heading out at the same time to what was an unusually calm Pacific Ocean. The sun had been up for only a half hour, and a cloudless sky was producing brilliant reflections off the water. The pelicans and myriad of other seabirds that inhabit Redondo's long breakwater were vying for breakfast. Their cries could be heard over the low rumble of Barry's diesel engines until he pushed the throttle forward to cruising speed. The boat planed and he matched Jonathan's speed at about 25 knots. We kept far back, but tracked his boat on the radar, keeping a good half a mile away. We were just another boat heading toward Catalina.

Before we got to the shipping lane that intersected the ocean between the mainland and the island, Jonathan's boat stopped moving. There were no cargo ships transiting the area that we could see visually or by radar, so that was apparently not the reason he was treading water.

"We'll slow down and get within visual," Barry said, motioning to the binoculars that were on the side of my seat. They were a pair of hefty Canon 18 X 50 marine binocs with image stabilization, which I knew cost over a grand, because they were a twin to the only relic left of Caerleon's death by fire.

"Love these binocs, Barry," I said, raising them and folding back the soft rubber eye covers so I could look through them with my sunglasses on.

"What can you see?" Barry asked, pulling back on the throttle, bringing the way off his engines until we were nearly stationary, with just a slight sway from the waves and current.

"I can see Jonathan on the cockpit deck. Looks like he's alone. I see one drum."

"Can you tell what he's doing?" Just as Barry finished speaking, two shots rang out. "Jesus, what was that?"

"He's holding a gun! He's standing back and appears to be shooting holes in the drum. What a jerk, he could put a bullet through his hull doing that."

Barry whistled. "Depends on what's in the drum – enough mass to stop the bullet or if it's liquid, it might come out the other side. Unbelievable. If he sinks, should we rescue him or leave him?" Two more shots rang out, then there was silence.

"He must be shooting near the top of the drum, which is above the boat's gunnel. Looks like he has put down his gun."

"I can guess what's coming," Barry said.

"He's rotating the drum over to the back of the boat, opening the gate," I added. What followed was exactly what we both predicted.

"There she goes, Barry. He's pushed the drum over. It's sinking, and he's gone back to the helm." We could hear his engines as Jonathan quickly revved up to speed and began making a long arc back toward Redondo."

"Let's head south of him, like we're continuing to cross the traffic lane toward Catalina," Barry said, pushing his twin engines into gear and leaning on the throttles. "Is the drum still above water? We could swing by it after he leaves the area if it hasn't sunk."

"Can't see it," I said. The waves were beginning to pick up, and like a human in the water who has gone overboard, it was nearly impossible to see where it was and whether it was still afloat or gone. "Let's circle back and see if there's any sheen on the water around where it went in – there might be one if it was waste oil or liquid chemicals."

"Roger," Barry said, marking the general spot on his GPS, and circling around. By this time Jonathan's boat was out of range, having headed back toward the mainland.

"No drum, no sheen," he said, driving a circular pattern near where the drum went into the water. I was peering through the binocs at the same time and couldn't see anything except waves.

"What the hell was he doing? Whatever he was dumping, it was illegal, even if it was just an empty drum," Barry said.

"Let's get back to the marina," I said. I'd like to see if he's cleaning up any kind of mess from the drum in his cockpit."

We drove back to the mainland and entered the harbor. Barry slowed down to five knots, and I went on deck to throw the fenders out on either side of the boat. Barry pulled slowly into his temporary slip, and I hopped off onto the dock and started securing lines to the dock cleats. I got back on board as Barry was shutting down the engines and picked up the binocs again to have a look at Jonathan's boat several docks over.

"I don't see anyone on the boat." I swung my view around the parking lot, looking for his car. "His car isn't where he parked it this morning either. He's left."

"Good, let's have a closer look," Barry said. We both disembarked and walked up the ramp of our dock, and over to Jonathan's dock. Barry's guest slip key opened the gate, and we walked down the ramp. There were no other boaters visible on the dock.

"Cockpit looks wet and clean. He's hosed it down from the looks of it, and no visible bullet holes. He's lucky," I said.

"Yeah, the guy didn't bother wrapping his water hose back around the dock box," Barry said, kicking the end of the hose that was lying on the dock beside the boat.

"Well, this doesn't tell us anything. I wish we'd had Gordie here with his zoom lens to capture what we saw him do. We need to document this guy's environmental crimes if nothing else."

"Right. I'll try to catch him leaving their Long Beach yard at the end of the day and see where he's off to for his evening's entertainment. Meanwhile, I have a friend in the Redondo PD. He's a top cop there. Why don't I give him a call and impart our observations. Maybe it will be enough to interest them."

"That would be great, Barry. Find out which agency might take the lead on something like this. Today was a good start anyways," I said, parting ways with him at the top of the dock ramp.

CHAPTER TWENTY-FIVE

It was just a few hours later when Barry phoned me from his surveillance on Jonathan.

"I saw him leaving the yard in his car and followed him all the way to your neck of the woods. He's gone into a restaurant in Santa Monica on Ocean Boulevard. I'm in the restaurant now. The bad news is that I think I'm burned in this vehicle, 'cause he took a circuitous route through Santa Monica for no apparent reason. He may have been checking if he had a tail."

"Good work that you were able to stay with him though. Can you switch vehicles for tomorrow and try to pick him up again?"

"Exactly."

"Did you get a look at whether he's alone in the restaurant?"

"He met up with a guy here and they've ordered food and drinks. I can't get close enough to hear their conversation without him getting a good look at me, so I won't be hanging around."

"Why don't I come by and try to follow him from the restaurant? I can borrow my dockmaster's car. He's always up for driving mine."

"That works, Mac. I'll move my car out of the parking lot but try to stay close enough to get a plate for his friend when he leaves or follow him where he goes for a while."

"I'll head down there now and text you when I arrive," I said.

The drive to Santa Monica in Bill's rather dusty Toyota took me fifteen minutes. I texted Barry on arrival, and positioned my car so I could see Jonathan's vehicle when he pulled out of the parking lot.

A moving surveillance in LA is much better accomplished with three or four cars and radios between them to coordinate, but if Jonathan headed home to his apartment in Venice, it would be easy to pick him up. He'd be taking Ocean Boulevard straight back there. If he went elsewhere, I'd have to see how long I could stay on him. Running red lights in order to stay on a tail was not an option.

"They're both coming out now. I'll see what I can get on his buddy if you can pick up on Jonathan," Barry said.

"Will do," I said.

"Be careful he doesn't see your face, Mac."

"I'm cleverly disguised with my hair up, hat and huge sunglasses."

"Ah, you'll look like everybody else in this town," Barry said, laughing. "Stay on the line with me," he added.

Jonathan pulled out of the lot and took a right turn down Ocean, the opposite direction of his apartment. I got on his tail with two cars between us. He followed the road and turned left on the California Incline, picking up Pacific Coast Highway going north.

"We're north on PCH. He's keeping to the speed limit, so it shouldn't be too hard unless I lose him at a red light at Entrada or Temescal Canyon, or Sunset if he goes that far."

"Okay, Mac. Let me know how it goes. I'll sign off now. I'm onto his buddy. He's heading east on Wilshire."

I edged up to be only one car behind Jonathan's Mercedes, and stayed with him through several lights. He moved over to the far-right lane just before Topanga Canyon Boulevard and signaled to turn. I moved over and stayed a hundred yards back, as I was the only car behind him in that lane. We both turned up into the canyon.

There was not much traffic on Topanga, being midday. It was not like rush hour when the multitudes of Los Angelenos who work on the west side or downtown head up the road from PCH to escape into what could be mistaken for another planet entirely. Much of Topanga, like Laurel Canyon, was a throwback to an undeveloped Los Angeles, with brush covered hills, canyons and cutbacks, funky second-hand stores, old and new cabins, and repurposed school buses parked on back roads.

Jonathan drove up into the center of Topanga and kept going. I nearly lost him at the only stop light in the middle of the town but caught up with him again just past the Theatricum Botanicum, which hosts outdoor plays all summer and maintains Woodie Guthrie's erstwhile cabin. If he kept going towards the valley, he would end up in Calabasas, if he didn't turn off before then. Near the top of Topanga, Jonathan turned right on an unmarked road, and I had to drive past, or I would have been right on his rear bumper. I kept going on the downhill side of the canyon, and turned around as soon as I could to head back up and follow him where he turned off.

The road was sparsely populated with houses, winding down the hill away from the boulevard, eventually turning into a dirt road. The scrub yards of the few houses I passed were littered with old cars and bikes. A couple houses had adjacent pipe stalls that were shades of dilapidated and had obviously not seen a horse for some time. I looked around for Jonathan's car as I drove, but as the road narrowed, I decided I should turn around before I ended up at a dead-end meeting him face to face.

I pulled into a dusty driveway and turned around. As I was heading back to the main drag, I saw his car parked, half hidden, on the back side of one of the houses. I kept going and ended up on Topanga Canyon Boulevard. I turned west and in less than a mile, drove into the parking lot of a small canyon café, and phoned Barry.

"He's in Topanga. I followed him to a house near the top and found his car parked there. I got the address. When I get back, I'll run some databases and see who owns it."

"Good work, Mac."

"Were you able to stay on his mate until he got somewhere?"

"Yeah, I followed him to an apartment complex off National. He parked his car there, went inside and a few minutes later, came out and got into a van and drove off. I've got plates and an address for you. I lost the van on Sepulveda Boulevard."

"Okay, thanks, I've got some homework to do. Got another call coming in." I hung up and picked up an incoming from Gordie.

"How are things going, Mac?"

"Good, I think. I've been following Jonathan and he's at a house at the top of Topanga. I'm going to leave him for now and head back to the marina."

"Meet up for dinner? I'm just about done for the day at the studio."

"Sure." We arranged a time and place, and I started the car to head down the hill. As I was about to turn into traffic heading west, Jonathan's car passed me going west. I turned east and drove back toward the location where I'd seen his car parked.

As I drove back toward the address where he'd been, I didn't pass a soul or another car. I pulled up in front of the house and got out. It was a one-story building, wood construction, and was probably 50 years or so old with a distinct lack of maintenance. The gutters were full of debris and the scrub vegetation around the property was untended and high - not a good idea in the canyon. At some point in the spring, the Topanga Fire Department would take heed when they did their inspections and left notices for residents. The fire department took brush clearance very seriously for good reason. Most of Topanga hadn't burned for many years, and it was primed for a disaster if a wildfire got out of control anywhere in the canyon.

There was no indication that anyone was habitually residing in the house — no well-tended driveway and the front walkway was overgrown. Some slats on the siding and roof were askew and the entire house needed paint. I wondered what Jonathan Chambers was getting up to here. I tried the front door, and it was locked. I walked around the back where a garden apparently used to be. It was just dirt, up to a wire fence around the yard that probably did little more than keep the coyotes away from the house.

There were several windows at the back of the house that were boarded up with plywood, and the back door had a padlock on the outside, which was strange. I returned to the front of the house and banged on the door, calling out to see if I got any response. The only reply was from a peacock who was wandering across the road. Before I knocked on doors of some of the neighbors, who may or may not know anything helpful since the houses were fairly spaced out, I wanted to do some background research. I needed to determine who owned it and see if I could connect them to Jonathan.

CHAPTER TWENTY-SIX

Fractions of time bend and surprise,
find me willing or coerced
by fortune or by design,
trying to find a reason
or a plan
where there is none.

"You've been busy," Gordie said, as we sipped our drinks at a restaurant on Washington Boulevard near the Venice pier. I filled him in on the surveillance of Jonathan's boat, the dumping of a drum, and the results so far of the tailing of Jonathan's car and that of his lunch buddy.

"When I get back to my laptop tonight, I'll plug the Topanga house address into the Recorder's Office website and see what I can find – deeds and tax info also."

"Is there any way we could get the Sheriff to open it up? What if Rowan has been in there? I know it's unlikely as there was no evidence that she left Catalina, but I guess I'm clutching at straws."

"They won't get a search warrant without some good cause shown. But I can knock on some neighbor's doors – see if anyone has noticed any activity at the house – and if I can find whoever owns it, I'll ask them what's up with it and find out how they know Jonathan."

"What about this other associate that Jonathan had lunch with? Maybe he'd have some answers."

"I'll see if I can put a name to him from the address and plates Barry got and try to find out if there's anything interesting about him."

"Every day that goes by…" Gordie stopped without finishing his sentence.

"I know." He grabbed my hand across the table and held it.

We went back to my studio after dinner and Gordie sat on the bed and caught up with his emails on his phone while I sat at the desk and sent another email update to Daniel and Brayden Collins. After that, I punched what I knew into the LA County public record websites, to see what I could come up with.

I obtained the assessor parcel number associated with the Topanga house address and searched around for everything from deeds and assessor records to the names of former and possibly current residents, as well as the names of their associates and relatives. I did not recognize any of the names of former or current owners who were listed, and Jonathan's name was not among them.

"He doesn't own it," I said to Gordie, as I continued my searches. "Unless he bought it very recently and it hasn't hit the records yet, but these are usually pretty much up to date."

"Who does own it?"

"A man named Brad Fulmer. Looks like he has owned it for at least 10 years. It's not his residence though. He has a property north of Montana Avenue in Santa Monica that's listed as his principal residence for the homeowner deduction. Topanga is likely a rental."

"Would you want to have a word with him? See if Jonathan is his current renter."

"I've got a number for him. I'll call him tomorrow. Question being why would Jonathan rent it when he has an apartment in Venice? And the Topanga house doesn't seem to be serving any purpose. It's not looking lived in or even like someone has been there regularly like if he used it as an office."

After I finished my online search for details on the Topanga house, I pulled up an email from Barry giving me the name and address of the man Jonathan had lunch with. I ran some preliminary databases on

Joe Thorn, which confirmed his address and showed that he was 45 years old and had a boat documented with the US Coast Guard. He was also an ex-con. The record listed a criminal record that resulted in a conviction and a brief stint in the county jail on drug charges ten years ago.

Joe Thorn's boat was a Cabo, an older model but a decent fishing platform. I also found a couple of civil lawsuits, a divorce, and a DUI conviction two years ago - long enough ago for him to have gotten his driver's license restored if he'd been a good boy. There were no hits on employment, so I was in the dark as to how he supported himself, but a closer look at the civil suits and divorce would likely shed some light, so I went into the Superior Court online site and searched the cases.

There were no online records for the divorce or one of the civil cases in LA County, as they were too old and would be in paper only in the archives, if they hadn't already been destroyed, but I pulled up the complaint for Packard Services vs. Thorn Hauling, Inc., and Joseph Thorn, Jr., filed three years ago. The subject matter of the civil dispute was a contract for hauling of recycling waste that Thorn had entered into with Packard Services on which he had reneged. Thorn was another lad in the hauling business. No wonder he was pals with Chambers.

I took a quick pass at socials for Joe Thorn, of which I found next to nothing. He wasn't keeping up with the tech, apparently. He had a Facebook account but hadn't posted anything other than one photo of himself holding up a large dead fish. I did a screen grab of the photo, so I'd at least know what he looked like.

Gordie stayed the night. I didn't think too much about it. I didn't tell him about Peter's situation, not even knowing yet how I was going to respond to it. I was just glad to have some company and it felt comforting to have him beside me.

In the morning, Gordie was off early to the studio, and I was on the phone following up with the boatyard and insurance company about Caerleon. I cringed when I heard she was getting towed to the scrap yard that afternoon, and if I wanted an opportunity to see if I could redeem anything from the boat, now was the time to do it. I drove over to the boat yard, feeling like I was going to a funeral.

The yard boss met me and walked me over to the stairs to climb up to a height where I could see what was left of her cockpit and cabin. "You be careful –she's a mess and it's not safe to put any weight on her."

"I'll just have a look," I said, knowing that anything that survived the fire inside the cabin would be inaccessible if not completely melted, and that would include my clothes and books.

I made my way up the stairs and looked over at the tangled black chaos that was Caerleon. The roof over the helm had melted and fallen down into the cockpit. The metal roof supports were only recognizable as blackened bars lying askew over a pile of roasted fiberglass.

"Yeah, what a debris field," I said, to the yardman who was holding down the base of the ladder.

"It'll cost the company well over five grand to haul and dismantle a boat this size. Some engine parts and metal will probably be recycled," he said.

"What a mess," I said, backing down the ladder to the tarmac.

I got back in the car and drove toward my apartment but decided to stop and have some lunch at a café in the marina. I sat outside on the patio and ordered a sandwich and a cup of tea. Over my lunch, I ruminated on my options post-boat. It might be a while before I got another boat. I might just take the insurance settlement, travel, and lead the digital nomad life for a while.

While at the café, I dialed Brad Fulmer, the owner of the Topanga house, and he answered on the first ring. I wasn't quite prepared with my thoughts on what to say to him when he picked up.

"Mr. Fulmer, I am doing some research on a property in Topanga that the records show you own..." Before I could say more, he interrupted me.

"It's not for sale. You're a real estate agent, I assume?"

"No, actually, a private investigator."

"That's a new one – usually it's an agent for someone who is looking to buy and tear it down and put up a McMansion on the property. What's your interest?"

"I'm just covering some bases really. I'm looking for a woman who disappeared a month ago and the person she was last seen with is a guy named Jonathan Chambers. He was up at the house in Topanga when I stopped by yesterday." That was a euphemistic way of saying he was under surveillance, but fortunately Fulmer didn't question it.

"Don't know that name. Is this guy Chambers some kind of suspect?"

"No, he's not a person of interest in her disappearance as far as the police are concerned, but we'd like to talk to him."

"My renter is Joe Thorn."

"Ah, thanks. I've run across that name. I think he's a friend of Chambers, which would explain why he was up at the house."

"I don't know Thorn, just rent to him. He answered a rental ad and paid 6 months in advance."

"How long ago did he start renting it?"

"About three months ago. He was planning on using it as a weekend retreat from the city, he said."

"When I went by yesterday, it didn't look like anyone was living there."

"I don't get involved, as long as a renter pays. I'll probably tear it down myself in a couple of years. I just don't have time to deal with it at the moment," he said.

"Just one more thing, Mr. Fulmer. I walked around the back and there was a padlock on the exterior of the back door, and a couple of windows boarded up. That seemed odd to me."

"Oh yeah? I didn't board up any windows or put a lock there. I hope Thorn didn't break some windows and drill a bunch of holes. That'll come out of his deposit."

"Well thanks, I appreciate your time."

CHAPTER TWENTY-SEVEN

Barry checked in by phone as I was driving back to my place after I spent a few hours doing another round of shopping to pick up some necessities for my barren studio. I stopped for a quick meal at a deli afterwards, and that settled for dinner. Barry reported that he had followed Jonathan in the morning to the Long Beach yard, where he parked his car then came out in a Chambers Environmental company truck.

"He's been toeing the line so far today, Mac. Looks like he might be on regular rounds. I stayed with him as far as two stops, one in City of Industry and one in Monrovia at a small industrial firm, where he picked up a couple of drums each. I lost him after that but will check back at the yard later and try to catch him after 5 PM."

"Thanks. By the way, Joe Thorn is the renter for the Topanga house – as of three months ago. The owner didn't know anything much else. Are there a lot of trucks coming and going from the yard?"

"Five other vehicles came out of the yard this morning around the time Jonathan left. Some bigger waste collection trucks, and a couple of smaller stake trucks. They all seem to head out around 7 AM."

"This guy is bugging me. What could he be dumping in the ocean?"

"Could be anything, Mac. If a customer doesn't want to pay the fee to dispose of haz waste in a proper Class 1 landfill, a waste hauler might keep it off the books and take a kickback to dump it elsewhere. Used to happen a lot. Not so much now that regulations and oversight are stricter."

"Yeah, I'm aware of that."

"Anything else come up with his lunch buddy, Thorn?" Barry asked.

"I ran database on him from the identifiers you gave me – he had a few lawsuits, divorce, and a 3-year-old DUI and a short vacation in the county jail on drugs. He has or had a company named Thorn Hauling, driving recycling waste according to one of the lawsuits, although he likely lost his license for a period of time after the DUI. And he has a boat, a Cabo fisher, so maybe he and Jonathan are fishing pals. Or doing God knows what at that Topanga house."

"Maybe, or they are business partners of some sort," Barry said.

"Or partners in crime. While you've got your boat in Redondo, see if you can find out if he keeps his boat in that marina."

"I'll ask around, check it out later. I'm spending the evening on the boat tonight."

When I got back to my apartment, Peter was waiting for me in the foyer.

"Who the fuck is this Derek Baker, Mac?" My ex was raising his voice to the point where the neighbors in my new apartment probably thought I was cheating on my husband, and he had just found out. It was more complicated than that.

"Calm down, Peter. That wasn't what I was expecting you came here to discuss," I said, ushering him inside the door. "In terms of Derek Baker, do you mean who is he in addition to a guy who is using your identity to get a tech job in America?"

"He couldn't get a loan in my name because of the credit freezes, but he tried. I had a call from the credit firm. He went to the Chevy dealer in Santa Monica and tried to buy a car. Got turned down, of course, when they tried to run credit and there was a freeze. I got a call from the credit company confirming it wasn't me."

"That's the good news," I said.

"Is this guy going to give up and get lost anytime soon?"

"I have no idea what he's up to, but I would like to know more. I'll get ahold of the Chevy dealer and see if they'll impart a local address for him. He must have filled out some forms."

"Thanks, Mac." Peter hugged me, unsolicited, but I didn't refuse. I was still too confused about him at this point to refuse.

"We'll talk about Jacob, Mac. I know it's a shock to you. It's a shock to me. But worse, obviously I was unfaithful to you earlier than you knew. It was a one-time deal. I'm so sorry. I thought since it was just a slip-up, a one-nighter, it didn't really matter. I guess it did."

"Yeah, it did. I'm not ready to discuss it, Peter. I'm still processing."

"Okay, Mac. Let's give it some space."

"Caerleon is going to her dismantling tomorrow. I went to see her up on the hard at the boatyard. I couldn't even see an entrance to the cabin. The roof was collapsed and the stairs into the cabin were gone. Everything I could see was just wet and ash."

"I'm so sorry. She was a fantastic ride when we had her." It didn't get past me that he said 'we.' Maybe he forgot that I lived on her alone for the two years after he dumped me and I dumped him.

"So much for my settlement in the divorce," I said, instantly regretting it. I don't know why I said it. Peter's reaction though, surprised me. Instead of going on the defensive, which he had every right to do in spite of the new revelations, he put his arms around me again.

"If you need a hand getting settled or finding a new boat, I'll help," he said. He took a step back and looked at me. "I mean I'll help if you need money." I wanted to hit him. Instead, I kissed him and pulled him over to the bed. Neither of us resisted.

I don't know if it was sex out of spite, or just sex because I missed him. I missed his body being something I had the right to touch, to have beside me. I missed his handsome face and the way he turned over in bed in the morning and checked his phone, and the way he drank his coffee in gulps, always heading out the door in a hurry wearing his flight uniform with his rolling suitcase. It all washed over me as we found our familiar rhythm and held each other like no time had passed. I knew it was going to hurt like hell in the morning, and it did.

"Sorry I don't have a full fridge worth of breakfast selections," I said. Peter was chugging his coffee at 8 AM, always up before me.

"That's okay." He wasn't looking me in the eyes.

"That was nice, last night," I said, and immediately wished I hadn't. So many regrets with this guy.

"Yeah, about that. I shouldn't have..." He put down his coffee and looked at that rather than me.

"No problem. Fun, anyways, Peter. You're still a piece of shit."

"I mean, shouldn't have because I'm getting a little serious with a woman I've been seeing in Denver on lay-overs. Not sure it'll last, but we're having a good time."

"Ah, okay, as in not fair to her, I guess you mean. Or maybe to all the others that I don't know about. Or maybe to your SON?"

"Right," he said. I took a deep breath and held it for a minute. There was nothing else to say.

We parted ways amicably, before I got into the privacy of my car and let out a scream.

CHAPTER TWENTY-EIGHT

Outside of time,
Fiction is the preferred medium.
But fantasy is a dreamstate
in sleep only.
Reality can burn like daylight.

Derek Baker pulled a hunting knife on me like he knew how to use it. I'd gotten a local address for him that afternoon from a kind salesman at the Chevy dealership who saw no point in protecting Baker's private information once his identity was deemed to be fake. The address was on 17th Street in Santa Monica, in a multi-unit apartment complex. I rang the gate buzzer once for the apartment number he'd listed, and when there was no reply, rang three other tenants until someone opened the gate. I went one flight up and knocked on his door. He opened it immediately, pulled me into the apartment, pushed me into a chair while brandishing the knife, which he pulled from a sheath strapped to the inside of his trouser leg. This was LA. It was surprising it wasn't a gun, but then he wasn't American.

"What the fuck, Derek? I just want to talk to you," I said, holding my hands up flat in front of me like a cop once told me to do when one is threatened with a weapon.

"You're a nosey fucking bitch," he said, some venom sliding off his Dublin accent.

"I'm looking for Rowan, and I would guess that you are too. We're not at cross purposes here, but you've got to stop using my ex-husband's identity. He's getting upset about it, and it's not going to work anyway. He's already put roadblocks up to stop you."

"I don't know anything about Rowan. I told you that last time you came uninvited to my place." Baker pulled a stool over and sat directly in front of me, one hand still holding the knife. I wanted to call him a lying sack of shit, but restrained myself, given that he had the upper hand.

"What's the point then? Why are you here, Derek?" He looked confounded for an instant, as though he wasn't sure what the point was himself. I had the feeling I was dealing with a confused guy, albeit a loose cannon type of guy. He regained his focus and held the knife up under my chin.

"Why don't you get the fuck out of my life, private investigator?"

"Yeah, I'll do that. Just put the knife down and I'll leave." He hesitated and backed away six inches. I still didn't have enough room to stand up.

"I'm going to find Rowan. But if you know anything that could help me know where to look, that would be helpful. I know you were looking for her in Catalina."

"I don't know where she is. She's probably dead." This wasn't going anywhere.

"Did you torch my boat?" I couldn't resist asking.

"What the fuck are you talking about?" He moved the stool back and stood up. His knife hand was shaking.

"Get out of here before I cut off a piece of ya." I stood up and made for the door, not looking back. I'd pushed him far enough.

CHAPTER TWENTY-NINE

It gets dark not long after dinner in LA in March. The weather is often gray and unsettled, unable to decide whether to be winter or spring. Gordie joined me after he finished work at what passes as a local bar. They don't make pubs in LA like they do in Ireland. They're far from cozy and most places selling alcohol are just noisy sports bars. To avoid the tv screens and bad acoustics, we sat on the patio with a heater going beside us.

"That wasn't smart, Mac," Gordie said, when I relayed to him my brief encounter with Derek Baker.

"You're right. The guy is unhinged. Rowan had two unpredictable guys in her life. That's two too many." I picked up my phone while Gordie worked on his pint. Barry answered after a couple of rings.

"How's it going Barry? Do you know Jonathan's whereabouts tonight?"

"Yeah, he's at a club downtown. I picked him up leaving after work and followed him to DTLA. I didn't go in — trying to save my face from looking familiar."

"What time did he get there?"

"Half hour ago."

"Good. I'm with Gordie, and I want to swing by the Topanga house again. Any contact with your Redondo PD man?"

"I spoke to him this afternoon. He sympathizes but said they don't have enough info to do anything at this point, but to keep him posted."

"Okay. Give me a shout when Jonathan leaves the bar if he's heading north. I don't want to run into any more pieces of shit today."

Gordie and I paid our bill and got in his rental for the trip to Topanga. Since it was a little past rush hour, the drive only took us 40 minutes. By the time we took the turn onto the unmarked road toward the house, it was well past dark. There was no activity to be seen at the house or the neighbor's houses. Not one light.

"Kinda creepy up here," Gordie said. He parked out front and I got out of the car with a flashlight. There were still no signs of humans having used the front door. I walked around back where Jonathan's car had been parked, with Gordie following behind me.

"The padlock is off the door," I said, shining my light in that direction. The back door was slightly open. I pushed the door in and called out asking if anyone was home, to dead silence.

"You're really going in there?" Gordie said.

"Yep. Just a little ways in."

I swept the flashlight across the floor inside the door. It was littered with debris that was mostly dirt. There were scrape marks across the floor, and on the other side of the room, several metal drums. They were partially rusted and had no tops. I walked over to them and shone the light inside.

"Empty," I said. Gordie came over beside me and inspected as well. There was a steel ramp leaned up against the wall, and in one corner of the room there was an old portable hand truck, some rags and smaller containers that were obviously old paint cans.

"Drums maybe been rinsed out. I don't see any residue," he said.

I continued further into the house and scanned the rooms briefly. There were no signs of occupancy. The kitchen was not fitted out with any pans or dishes and looked completely unused. There was scant furniture in what was probably the living room, and a master bedroom. The bathroom was dirty and was the only room that looked like it had been used in recent memory.

"Let's get out of here, Mac. I don't like this." I followed him back the way we came and out the door.

"This place has been used to store barrels and whatever else, but that seems about it," I said, getting in the car.

"Jonathan and Joe Thorn are using it for something, and I doubt they're filing the required waste manifests with the state of California for whatever they're transporting."

Gordie drove us back down the hill and along PCH, through Santa Monica and Venice to the marina. Traffic was light and the summer tourists were not yet standing dangerously mid-street on Pacific near Muscle Beach to take selfies under the Venice sign.

Gordie dropped me off with apparent regret that I wasn't inviting him up, but I hadn't quite shaken off the emotions from being with Peter the night before, or the smell of Peter that seemed to permeate my flesh despite my morning shower.

CHAPTER THIRTY

In the morning, I packed an overnight bag to drive down to San Pedro to catch the first Flyer. I was going back to Catalina. As it turned out, I wouldn't need to take the Flyer.

As soon as I had loaded my bag in the trunk and started the car to drive to San Pedro, Barry called. "Jonathan disappeared yesterday, I lost him after work, and he reappeared this morning. His car wasn't at his apartment early, so I drove to the Long Beach yard. He just pulled out in a van and looks to be heading to Redondo. If you can get here in time, we can take another joy ride out into the bay."

"I'm already in my car. Be there as soon as possible, but if he takes off before I get there, head out after him anyways and I'll catch up with you after. I'm going to call Gordie and see if he can join us with his zoom lens."

"See you soon hopefully."

I phoned Gordie and he agreed to head out immediately and join us. The drive to Redondo was sluggish in morning traffic, but both of us got there minutes apart before Jonathan and Barry headed out to sea. Since Barry's boat was on a neighboring dock, it wasn't likely Jonathan would see either of us, but I didn't want to take any chances. I called Barry before I got out of my car to assess Johnathan's whereabouts, so I wouldn't run into him.

"He's on his boat, so the coast is clear. Come on down. I left the gate ajar for you."

I grabbed my bag from the trunk, rather than leave it in the car, and joined Gordie in the parking lot to go down the gangway. Barry had his engines running and had already cast off the lines when we stepped into his cockpit. He pulled out slowly and headed into the main channel.

"He's still on the boat, but I want to get in front of him this time, just in case he recognizes my boat from last trip and sees me follow him out again." I took a front seat, pulled on a baseball cap and put Barry's high-powered binocs beside me on the seat. Gordie sat behind me with his camera on the seat beside him.

"Did he load any cargo?" I asked.

"He rolled a drum down from the van to the boat on a dolly, so maybe a repeat performance. He was also getting his dingy in the water, looks like for a tow, so he's maybe going to the island.

I pulled in the fenders on both sides of the boat as we passed more docks on the way out of Basin 2 to the main channel. At the docks, which were part of the Port Royal Marina, Barry pointed out another sport fisher type boat that I recognized as a Cabo. It was smaller than Jonathan's, maybe a 28-footer with a cabin. I took a photo of it with my phone.

"I have it on good authority that is Joe Thorn's boat, Fish Winder. Haven't seen him in it yet, Barry said."

We were outside and south of the harbor entrance when Jonathan's boat emerged and sped up, heading toward the island. He was towing his 12-foot hard-bottomed inflatable behind his boat. Through the binocs, I could see the 55-gallon drum in his cockpit. He had it lashed to the gunnel with some rope, obviously to stop it from sliding around from the boat's motion.

Barry kicked up his speed in what were quiet seas with barely 2-foot swells, and we followed in the same general direction.

"He's taking a different heading than last time. Going directly to Catalina." There were several other boats heading that way as well, likely going to the island for the weekend, so we had some cover.

Jonathan didn't stop until he got to Avalon Harbor. While he caught a mooring, we hovered outside the harbor to see what would happen next. The sun was just coming out from behind the clouds, and the blue water started sparkling and reflecting rays off the moored boats. The surrounding hills were a deep green. Avalon was its picture-perfect best.

"He's getting into the dingy," I said, looking through the binocs.

"Maybe going to visit the Chambers' yard here. I don't think either of us should try to follow him on land at this point. Let's throw down the hook, have some lunch, and see if we can catch him leaving. There's tuna salad in the fridge."

Barry set down the anchor in some deep water outside the harbor moorings, then we had a leisurely lunch and waited for close to two hours. I checked with the binocs periodically to look for him moving his dingy from the dock. Finally, he reappeared, got in his dingy and went back to his boat. He wasn't alone this time.

"It's Joe Thorn, Barry."

"Ah, interesting. Thorn didn't come over on his own boat. Maybe came on the Flyer and needed a ride home."

Barry started his engines and weighed the anchor, then we followed Jonathan at a good distance when he headed out of the harbor, both boats setting a course toward Redondo. While Barry piloted, Gordie and I set up a couple of rods in the fixed holders on the gunnel, to make it look like we were fishing.

A half hour into the ride, Jonathan slowed and stopped. We were well back, but it was apparent from his boat's position on Barry's radar that he wasn't moving, so we did the same. There were a couple of sailboats in our vicinity, one heading toward the island under sail, and the other motoring back toward the mainland, plus other large motor yacht transiting the area, but none were close enough to Jonathan's boat to pay any attention to what he was doing.

Looking through the binocs, I could see the two men on the cockpit deck, and they seemed to be doing something with the drum. Gordie was ready with the camera and taking some snaps.

"They're moving it over to the gunnel hatch. There she goes," I said, watching the men push the drum into the water. They stood there watching it as it slowly sank. Gordie continued taking photos.

"Alright, let's hang here until they've left in case the thing doesn't sink entirely or leaves a sheen behind." We watched Jonathan motor off toward the mainland, his inflatable dingy bobbing behind Flight Risk on a tow line, and then we got as close as we could to his last known position. I acted as lookout to make sure our boat wasn't going to hit a partially submerged drum. Barry marked our location on his GPS to capture the latitude and longitude of the area.

"I don't see the drum or a sheen on the water," Gordie said, looking through his zoom. But can we get closer?"

Barry motored closer to the approximate spot where the drum went overboard. "What do you see now," he said.

Gordie peered over the side. "Some kind of sheen on the water. Small patch of dark liquid. Looks like molasses."

"Looks like blood," I said, feeling sick to my stomach. There were a few bubbles popping up into a thin pool of dark liquid, about the size of two saucepans on the surface of the water. It was dispersing quickly in the wave action.

"Can we get a sample," Barry said.

"No telling what it is. Could actually be oil. It's disappearing too fast to grab, I think," Gordie said, taking more photos.

"Alrighty, let's head home. We have the photos at least."

"Whatever Chambers is up to, Joe Thorn is deep in it," I said. I want to know more about Thorn – what he's doing on the island. Instead of going back with you to Redondo, can you drop me off in Catalina?"

"Sure thing."

"I've got my overnight bag, so I can stay in a hotel and take the Flyer home tomorrow, but I want to check something out on the island." Gordie looked at me.

"Do you want me to join you?"

"I'll be okay, Gordie. You guys are just a phone call and an hour or so away if I need back-up"

"Don't go stirring up any hornet's nests, Mac," Gordie said.

"I'll be staying on my boat tonight, Mac. If you need me to head back to the island, I'll be there. And meanwhile, Gordie, if you can get me those photos that would be great."

"When we get back to Redondo, I'll transfer them to you," Gordie said.

Barry turned back toward Avalon to drop me off. The afternoon chop was picking up, sending spray over the windshield as we motored back to Avalon Harbor in the increasing swells.

"I'll send the photos to my man at the PD and see what he thinks. I hope we have enough evidence from the photos to interest them now."

"See what he says, but he'll probably just refer us to a federal agency. We were more than 3 miles out in international waters, not the harbor."

"Someone needs to figure out what they're dumping into the Pacific Ocean," Barry said.

CHAPTER THIRTY-ONE

I didn't really have a plan for when I got on land in Avalon, but I needed some time and space to put the pieces that I had so far in the investigation into some kind of order in my head, and Catalina seemed to be the place to do that. Rowan was still missing, a week had gone by and other than gleaning some miscellaneous information about her stalker and the last man she was with, who was likely violating hazardous waste regulations, I'd made no progress. The one new element that I was armed with was a photo of Joe Thorn and a picture of his boat. Thorn was connected to Chambers, and I wanted to know more.

I headed to a café along the main drag and ordered a cup of tea. Avalon seemed sleepy, like it had barely woken up from the winter. The seagulls were making more noise than the rest of the town.

I walked over to the dingy dock and asked a guy who was running the shore boat when Sandy would be on duty, and he said she wasn't due to show up for another hour to work the boats. I took a leisurely walk toward the casino and up the hill on Chimes Tower Road to the Zane Grey Hotel. Their bar was open, and being the start of happy hour, I ordered something stronger than tea and took a seat on their patio overlooking the harbor next to a heater. The grey sky was darkening, with some rain clouds hovering in the air offshore. I was setting down my glass on the counter when I noticed a familiar figure enter the patio at the opposite end. He was with another man, and they were carrying beer glasses. They sat down and engaged in conversation without a glance my way. The man I recognized was Greg Chambers. Being the inevitable shit disturber that I am, I gave him five minutes before I walked over to their table.

"Hi Greg, do you remember me?"

"You're the one who was making all sorts of trouble for my brother. I'd hoped I wouldn't see your face around here again."

"If that was one of your guys in the white pick-up truck who crashed into my golf cart after I visited you at the yard, I'm sorry to tell you that attempt to intimidate me has failed."

"Don't know what you're on about," he said, swigging his beer. He was smiling and looking at his colleague, who was also smiling. Lot of smiling going on.

"Do you know Joe Thorn? He seems to do some business with Jonathan."

"Not going to answer any of your questions. You'd better think about getting off this island while you can."

"Yeah, maybe that's a good idea, enjoy your drinks." I said, taking my leave. I paid my check and left the hotel, then walked down to the main street. If Gordie had been there, he would have kept me from stirring the waters.

When I got back to Crescent Drive, I went onto the Green Pier and looked for my shore boat captain. Sandy was just tying her boat up when I found her. She hopped up on the dock when she finished with the lines.

"Hi Mac, nice to see you back. How's Caerleon – I haven't seen her come into the harbor."

"Bad story, Sandy. She got torched. Burned beyond recognition by we don't know who."

"Oh man, that's horrible! I hope no one was hurt?"

"No one was injured, just my heartbreak."

"So sorry, Mac. I don't know if it's insensitive to ask, like with someone whose dog just died, but are you getting another boat?"

"Don't know yet, but if I go that direction, I'll probably get a sailboat. Grin and bear those six hour trips over here from Marina del Rey."

"That really sucks. About Caerleon. Not the part about getting a sailboat."

"Yep. Hey, I have another photo to show you. I'm still on the trail of the woman who went missing last month."

"Sure, show me what you've got. I'm sorry to hear the girl hasn't turned up." I pulled my phone out of my pocket and showed her the photo of Joe Thorn.

"This guy, whose name is Joe Thorn, has a Cabo sport fisher – about a 28-footer maybe." I swiped to the next photo and showed her the boat.

"Any chance you remember him being on the is-land around the time Rowan Collins went missing?"

"Ah, that's hard to say timing-wise, Mac, but I do know this boat. She's called Fish Winder. This guy Thorn is around pretty often. I don't know what he does but he comes in and out of the harbor at least five times a month. Maybe has a dingy – not sure about that. Sometimes he takes the shore boat."

"Thanks, that's helpful. Ever seen him with any of the guys from Chambers Environmental?"

"Yeah, now that you mention it, I've seen him with the brother, Greg, a few times, and maybe Jonathan too. I think he has a house on the island. I remember him one time around the holidays when I brought him ashore, we were talking about the weather, and he said something about his roof being damaged in the big windstorm we'd just had."

"Ah, okay thanks."

"Good luck on a new boat, Mac. I hope that works out for you."

"Me too. See you around," I said, heading back to the main drag.

Rather than get a hotel, I decided to catch the last express boat back to the mainland, as I couldn't think of anything to do that wouldn't get me into more trouble. I needed to do some more research to find out where Joe Thorn's house was on Catalina, and I needed my laptop for that. I walked over to the Flyer dock, bought a ticket at the booth, and sat down on the low concrete wall near the gangway to check my phone while I waited for the boat. There was a text from Gordie, so I called him back.

"Where are you, Mac?"

"I'm in Catalina but coming back on the Flyer. My car is in Redondo. Is there any chance you might be able to come by and pick me up when I get in from the Flyer in San Pedro?"

"Sure. I'm still in Redondo so I'll swing down to San Pedro and get you. I was wrapping up here. I've been hanging out with Barry for a bit. What time do you get in?"

"Seven-thirty, if that works for you."

"I'll be there."

The seas were rough on the way back, with the steel hull of the boat pounding, trying to catch up with the wave crests, but failing and rattling through the troughs. I read the news on my phone until I ran out of cell signal, then watched the sea spray against the windows. I felt like I was buried in the swells, on the underside of a depression that I couldn't put my finger on. It was the lack of progress on the case, the threats, the ex. Maybe the sex with the ex. I went to the bar and got a glass of white wine in a plastic cup. I hate drinking wine out of a plastic cup. I don't know why I bothered.

Gordie was waiting for me when we disembarked. I spent most of the ride filling him in on the status of the case and the excitement that he'd missed regarding my interaction with Greg Chambers.

"You think you'll get some law enforcement scrutiny of Chambers with those photos of him and Thorn dumping a drum?"

"I hope so. Someone has to take that and run with it. Not much else I can do, and I don't even know if it has any relevance to my case. Rowan could have gone in the water in Avalon and just not come up for all we know at this point."

"What's next, Mac? There must be something else we can do."

"I want to take a deeper dive with Joe Thorn, and given the lack of leads, I need to call Rowan's father in Belfast, who is underwriting all the fun we're having here, to see how much further he wants me to take it."

When Gordie dropped me off at my car in Redondo, I begged off a late dinner or further entertainment and headed back to my apartment.

CHAPTER THIRTY-TWO

When I got to the foyer of my apartment complex, my erstwhile dockmaster, Bill, and two cops were standing there talking. I didn't like the looks of it, especially since the uniforms must have been on overtime. I started a quick mental inventory of every law I'd recently broken.

"Mac, can we come up to your place and talk?" Bill said. I had one of those feelings you get when you watch a cop show on television and you're anticipating whatever dark deed the cops were tasked with.

"Sure, come on up, I said, getting into the elevator with the three of them, carrying my overnight bag. I wondered if I should make a run for it while I still could, but it was too late. They were in blue, not the beige outfits of the marina's LA County sheriffs. These were LA City cops. I unlocked my door and ushered them into my sparce surroundings.

"Sorry about the lack of seating arrangements. Bill might have mentioned that I've just lost my live-aboard and haven't had time yet to do any furniture shopping." The four of us were standing, given that the small couch I had wouldn't fit all of us.

The taller and bulkier of the two guys pulled out his ID. "Officer Grady, LAPD. I understand you know Peter Girard. Bill was explaining to us that he's your ex-husband and he used to own the boat that just burned. We thought you may be able to direct us to his next of kin if you're not it."

"Yes, Peter's my ex-husband. What are you talking about?"

"There was a vehicle accident on the 10 freeway. It involved a fatality – the driver of one of the cars. We found his wallet with his driver's license, so we believe Peter Girard is the deceased."

"Do you mind if I sit down for a moment," I said.

"Please, sit down," Officer Grady said. The couch was sufficient to fit myself and Bill. He sat down beside me and looked at me with consternation. "There was a car fire, so the deceased individual is not able to be identified visually, and the car he was driving was stolen, so we aren't able to ID him from vehicle records."

"It's not Peter," I said. Both cops and Bill looked at me sympathetically.

"I'm not – it's not what you think. I know for a fact that Peter left on a flight to Denver yesterday and isn't coming back until the end of the week. His identity was hijacked, people trying to get loans in his name. It definitely has to be a person who is using his credentials, and I know who that might be."

"What can you tell us?" Grady said.

I pulled out my phone and looked through my photos. I pulled up the photo of Derek Baker.

"I think this might be your man. He's over here from Ireland and recently produced a fake California driver's license in Peter's name when he applied for some remote work with a tech firm in Santa Monica. They hired him based on the credentials he provided saying he was Peter Girard." Officer Grady took a photo of Derek Baker with his phone while his colleague was taking notes. After he did that, I dialed Peter.

"Peter," I said, when he picked up. I felt a rush of relief. Even though I knew he wasn't the dead man, I wiped my eyes with my sleeve. "Thank God you picked up. There are a couple of LA City police here. Someone with a driver's license in your name was just killed on the 10 in an accident. I think it's Derek Baker."

"Christ, Mac! I'm still in Denver."

"I know – here, talk to Officer Grady." I handed my phone to the officer, and they exchanged information. He handed the phone back to me and I signed off with Peter.

"Give me a shout when you're back, Peter. I want to see your corporeal presence. Just to be sure," I said. We hung up. Officer Grady handed me a card with a phone number on it.

"Have you met this Derek Baker in person?"

"I had the unfortunate experience a couple of times. He has a reputation for stalking, cybercrime, and identity theft. I guess you can add car theft to that list."

"We may want to speak with you further, Miss, when we have more information."

"Okay." I reached into my purse and pulled out my business card for him.

The cops left; Bill stayed. We walked over to the Marriott and sat on the second-floor bar overlooking the marina.

"What if the late Derek Baker was involved with the disappearance or death of my subject? Now that really is a dead end."

"Isn't this the guy you thought might have torched Caerleon?"

"A possible suspect although there is no evidence linking him to it. Not yet anyways."

Bill and I sipped our drinks and watched the airplanes on the horizon as they were lining up to land at LAX. I have a habit of counting them. On a clear night, there might be as many as seven or eight visible at a time, evenly spaced lights in the sky that you could see from the marina. It was called the necklace of LA. Whoever came up with that allegory was right. It's urban bling, reminding us that we live on a beautiful spinning celestial rock overseen by flying things.

CHAPTER THIRTY-THREE

The next morning was spent catching up with correspondence and looking for records on Joe Thorn's property on Catalina. Through the Recorder's Office website, I found that he owned a 1200 square foot house in Avalon with two bedrooms and one bath, which he'd bought 10 years ago. It was not his primary residence, so he was possibly renting it during the high tourist season. I made a note of the address in my phone.

As I was shuffling emails, Gordie checked in and said he was tied up on a shoot. My boat insurance company also called to say my claim was being processed. Then Officer Grady called.

"The body of the man who had Peter Girard's identification has been confirmed as Derek Baker," Grady said. "Do you have any further information on his next-of-kin in Ireland or addresses, in addition to the Santa Monica apartment you've already given us?"

JULIE BERGMAN

"I have an address for a flat in Dublin where he was staying with a flat mate. I don't have any family information for him," I said. I pulled up the address from my computer and gave him the details.

"He is now a suspect in your boat fire, Ms. Brody, based on documents that were found at his apartment here. He had made notes with the name of your vessel and marina address. We may know more when the contents of his laptop are reviewed."

"He pulled a knife on me the last time I saw him. Nothing he did would surprise me. I think I'd spooked him enough to want to destroy my personal effects."

I got up from my apartment-sized desk and made a cup of tea, trying to process all the things that were happening. I sat down again at the computer and started a list of everything I needed to do regarding the boat and the current case. My cell rang again. It was Peter.

"I'm glad you're alive Peter, but that's as far as I can go."

"I'm so effing sorry for everything, and that I didn't tell you about my son as soon as I heard that I have one."

"Your affairs, your women, your son. Not my circus."

"I didn't do it to hurt you, Mac, I need you to understand that."

"We had such promise, Peter, as a couple. And a few good years, I guess."

"I hope you will meet Jacob and get to know him. I'm going to see him tomorrow. I'm scared shitless."

"As I said, your circus. Can't help you there."

"But don't you want to meet him and get to know him? He's your son too, in a way."

"He's not my son. He had a mother and has a father. It's got nothing to do with me. I hope he's a great kid and that he doesn't hate you as much as I do right now."

There was silence on the other end of the line, which I felt compelled to end.

"Good luck, Peter." He signed off quietly.

I turned off my computer and packed a small overnight bag. I had things to do that thankfully didn't involve my ex-husband. I drove down to San Pedro and got on the Catalina Express again to the island. The sun was coming out as I was arriving in Avalon Harbor, and the weather was turning milder. I shed the jacket I was wearing and wrapped it round my waist as I disembarked at the dock. Then I walked over to the shore boat dock and found Sandy.

"Hey Sandy, any chance you've seen that guy Thorn and his Cabo coming in?"

"Not a sign of him or Flight Risk, and I've been working the boats so I would have seen him."

"Thanks, good to know," I said, and headed over to Crescent Street and rented a golf cart.

Thorn's house was on Tremont Street, off Avalon Canyon Road that led up to the Botanical Garden. I parked my cart across the road. The house was one story with a weathered front. What was left of the paint showed white wooden siding with a faded blue edge ringing the two front windows. There was no driveway, only a low slatted fence around a scrub yard, with a broken gate leading to the front door. I went to the door and knocked. There was no response. My phone rang as I walked back to the golf cart. It was Barry.

"Hi Mac, I shared the photos of Chambers and Thorn deep sixing the barrel in the water with the head cop in Redondo last night. He is referring it to the feds and Coast Guard Sector LA-Long Beach. He said Redondo PD would only be involved if something washed up on their shore, not a suspicious dumping in international waters. Not sure how soon anyone might act on it, but at least we've got it in motion."

"Unlike six feet under, it's six fathoms down in a metal can. There's something in those barrels they don't want anyone to know about," I said.

"Reminds me of the well-known fact that a whole lot of drums of waste toxics were dumped into the ocean between Long Beach and Catalina years ago. Now they're sitting on the bottom rusting and leaking. God knows how anyone is going to fix that situation," Barry said.

"Right. The ocean bottom is very deep there. There's even an old, discontinued dump site on the chart for that area."

"Yeah, I always wondered about that. Probably military."

"Are you on Chambers today?"

"Yeah, Mac, that's the next thing I was going to report. He got on his boat and headed out a couple of hours ago. I couldn't follow him as I'm tied up with some family stuff this afternoon."

"Did he have any drums on board?"

"Two drums, and no telling where he was headed."

"Did you happen to see whether Joe Thorn's boat is still in the slip?"

"It's not. It was gone when I got to my boat this AM, before Chambers even left. I have no idea when Thorn might have gone out – could have been yesterday. Where are you today?"

"I'm back on the island. I wanted to check out Thorn's house here. I found it – looks like no one is home, and his boat hasn't been seen in the harbor today."

"Alright, be careful Mac. There are two unpredictable guys in the wind."

"Will do, thanks Barry. How long have you rented the guest slip for in Portofino Marina?"

"Another week, then if there's no further need, I'll move her back to Marina del Rey."

"Alright. Let's hold off on further surveillance until I have a chat with our benefactor to see if he wants us to continue looking for Rowan. I need to keep him in the loop on the budget. Send me an invoice to date, and then I'll call him."

"It'll be in your email by this evening."

"I hate not having anything to tell him, but we've just been going in circles with these jokers, and now it looks like Derek Baker might be dead in a car wreck yesterday in LA."

"Jesus, Mac. Bad luck for him. He should have stayed in Ireland."

CHAPTER THIRTY-FOUR

There is beauty in fire-scarred hillsides
when the deer and jackrabbits return.
The hawks begin again stalking prey
from above.
The singed scrub oaks that grasped onto survival
begin to green,
showing nature's renewing face,
instead of its destruction.

After the call with Barry, I turned the golf cart around and headed up to the Botanical Gardens. If nothing else, I was going to enjoy the rest of the morning while I mulled over what other actions I could take before I called Daniel Collins and told him we were at an impasse.

There was scant activity on the road up to the 40-acre gardens, so it didn't take me long to notice that either I had a tail behind me, or someone was just heading in the same direction. But it wasn't a cart, it was a white pickup.

I drove the rest of the way up to the garden entrance and parked. Whoever might be driving the pickup would have to follow me on foot if they wanted to have a chat. I walked through the Avalon Canyon, past a huge array of native plants and succulents, and up to the Wrigley Memorial, a stone building at the top of the gardens with a Catalina tile fountain at its base.

The memorial was built in 1934 for William Wrigley, Jr., the patron of modern-day civilization on the island. There was a marble-floored circular tower, with a view all the way to the mainland on a clear day. It was one of my favorite places in California, and I'd always dreamed of sharing that view with a friend and a bottle of wine someday. When I finally had the chance a few years ago, it was with a friend who tragically died not long after, so in my mind it was a memorial to them rather than to Wrigley, Jr.

While I went for a stroll, the white truck remained parked in the lot at the base of the Botanical Garden. Barry phoned back just as I arrived at the memorial and turned around to take in the clear view over Avalon.

"Mac, you need to know this. Are you somewhere you can talk?"

"I'm at the Wrigley Memorial. It's nice up here, and amazingly, I've got enough cell signal to hear you."

"I just had a call from my pal at Redondo PD. It's pretty crazy. The FBI have had an eye on Chambers

Environmental people for a while. There was some connection between the company and a migrant smuggling operation in Mexico."

"Jesus, that's something that hadn't occurred to me."

"They're getting search warrants for Chambers' Long Beach and Catalina yards, and their trucks and boats."

"Christ, Barry, worse than I imagined."

"Right. This could get dicey very quickly. You need to get back here and out of the way of any of those guys. It's possible there was a dead body in that drum that went over the side."

Barry paused, and I added, "And Rowan could have been one of them."

"I wasn't going to say that, Mac, but she could have been killed on the island and transferred to Jonathan's boat from one of the small coves away from Avalon, and no one would have seen it."

"Transferred for disposal. I hate that word, Barry."

"I'm coming over there to get you on my boat. I'll phone Gordie. He can join me if he gets here in time."

"Let me know when you get into the harbor, and I'll grab a shore boat out to you."

"Please stay out of sight until I get there, Mac. With the federales closing in on Chambers, all hell could break loose."

I walked down the steps from the memorial and back through the gardens toward the parking lot. I didn't see the white pick-up truck where it had stopped before, which was a relief. I sat down in my golf cart and was about to turn the key when I was grabbed from behind by the neck. Something was held over my mouth. I struggled but suddenly my vision was fading. I tried but couldn't move my arms. They felt weighed down.

That was all I knew until becoming aware of the splashing noise of waves on a hull. I was dreaming that I was back on Caerleon, pleasantly falling asleep while on anchor at the island.

CHAPTER THIRTY-FIVE

My happy dream of sleeping on Caerleon started to fade. I kept trying to get back to it. I wanted to be on my boat, waking up in the V-berth next to Peter, floating on the blue waters of Catalina, with the seabirds and waves the only sounds. Before the divorce, before the fire.

I had trouble breathing, and for a minute, the dream turned to me being trapped in the V-berth alone while Caerleon went up in flames around me. I tried to shake myself awake to escape the nightmare, but my body was restrained.

My vision was foggy but began to clear. I was lying on my side and for the first few minutes all I could hear was my heart pounding loudly in my ears. My hands were restrained in front of me with a plastic tie, which was tight and chaffing, and there was tape over my mouth. I was in the small cabin of a boat, on the floor, partially under the salon table, which was blocking my view of the rest of the cabin. I tried to move my legs, but they were tied together around the ankles.

I heard another voice through my haze, but it wasn't registering. Then it got louder.

"Can you help? Who are you?"

I tried to answer but all I could do was make some groaning sounds, the tape over my face muzzling my words. I wriggled further from the table so I could see the front of the cabin beside the galley. There was another body on the floor that was coming into view as my vision started to improve. I realized I could reach the duct tape that was plastered over my mouth and yank it off. Stupid perp should have tied my hands behind me. I pulled at the tape and gasped at the sudden shock of losing some surface skin cells in the process.

"Are you okay?" The disembodied voice took shape. There was a woman across from me, similarly secured. I couldn't see her clearly enough yet to make out details, but I heard the accent, and felt a sudden rush of emotion. My confusion was starting to fade.

"How did we get here... who?" I asked quietly, not sure whether we were alone.

"I've been kept for weeks in a cabin. They moved me to a car, then to a small boat and then here." She was crying through her words. It was obvious who my cell mate was.

"Rowan," I said, through the tears of my relief. It didn't matter that we were tied up and heading to some unknown end. I'd found her.

"You were brought here in a truck at the same time, but you were out cold."

"Your father – he hired me to look for you when the police couldn't find you."

"Oh my God." That was all she said. It was enough.

"Can you move – maybe reach a galley drawer - a knife?" I was too far away from her and too disorientated to manage moving closer.

"I'll try," she said. Just as she spoke, the boat shuddered with forward motion, spinning around and picking up power. The cabin door to the cockpit was shut, with no way to see who was at the helm controls. The movement knocked her down as she was trying to get to her knees. She struggled again to swing her legs around under her. I heard, rather than saw, the rattle of a drawer being opened and the sound of steel against steel, then a clatter to the teak floor.

"Got it. I can't cut my hands loose but my feet…"

In the space of 10 seconds, Rowan had cut the tie around her ankles and gotten her feet under her to get to me. I held out my hands, and with hers still tied together, she held the kitchen knife in one hand and sawed at the cable tie that was securing mine until it snapped.

"You're bleeding a little, sorry," she said, as a small stream of blood dripped from my wrist where the knife had nicked me. I took the knife from her and cut her hands free, then my ankles.

"Who brought us here, Rowan, was it Jonathan?"

"Yeah, and some other guy. But I think it's only Jonathan on the boat. The other guy took the dingy off somewhere."

"We've got to get control of this boat. Does Jonathan have a gun with him?"

"He pulled one on me to force me into the house when he locked me up. I don't know if he has it with him. But it's not what you think."

"What do you mean?"

"He was trying to keep me safe. He said he cared about me."

"What?"

"I know he's a bad guy, but he was trying to save my life. He said that because I found out what they were doing with the dead people, his brother was going to kill me. He had to hide me from his family until he could figure out how to get me off the island without anyone knowing I was still alive."

"How did you find out about the bodies?"

"I heard bits of a conversation about it when he was on his cell phone on his boat, on the way over here. He didn't know I was in earshot. Then there was a big open drum on board. It was empty but smelled terrible and had what looked like some blood in it. I put that together with the conversation I'd heard, and I confronted him. He went berserk."

"Jonathan's not going to play nice, Rowan. He's going to be desperate. The Feds are onto them, and he has probably heard about it by now. He may put this boat on autopilot any moment and come down to silence one or both of us."

"He has two empty drums on the deck. That's not a good sign," she said.

"Fuck," I said.

CHAPTER THIRTY-SIX

The boat was dancing against some slow swells, with the engine revving in the troughs. The noise was exacerbating the ringing in my head left over from whatever chemical was used to put me under.

I staggered to my feet, holding myself up against the table, still grasping the knife and looking around to see what else we could use to defend ourselves. In the instant that I took to take stock of the cabin, the door from the cockpit swung open and I saw two legs, then the rest of Jonathan Chambers come down the steps.

I didn't wait for an introduction. I jumped him, knife still in hand. Both of our bodies crashed to the floor, struggling. He grabbed the wrist of my knife hand, pushing it away from himself and in the process plunged it into my left shoulder. I recoiled from the searing pain as he pulled it out and grabbed me, twisting my excruciatingly throbbing shoulder, shouting at the same time.

"You fucking bitch. You've ruined everything. I was trying to save her."

He held me down with one hand on my neck, while swinging the knife around in the other. I chocked from the pressure on my neck, then he eased it up and knelt over me.

"You've got a fucked way of trying to save someone."

"You're coming up on the deck with me and then you're going deep. I've got a drum just the right size for you."

Jonathan yanked me partially to my feet and shoved me toward the stairs to the cockpit, bashing my head against the stairs in the process.

Rowan stopped him cold. I heard a dull thud behind me as she hit him on the head with a metal grate from the stovetop. He pulled me back down the stairs on top of him as he was falling, then there was another thud as he hit the deck. I rolled off him onto my back on the floor.

"Christ you've been stabbed," Rowan said, stepping over him to get to me. I closed my eyes, took a deep breath and held it for a moment. I started to sit up and Rowan took my good arm to help me.

"Is he bleeding?" I asked.

She looked over at Jonathan's prone body. "Not much. Let me see your shoulder." I pulled my hand away from where I was trying to stop the blood.

"Can you tie him up with something – anything. Make sure he's still out cold but breathing. I've got to get to the helm and the radio."

I stood up shakily, with her hand supporting me. She picked up the knife from where he'd dropped it.

I climbed the two steps up into the cockpit and sat down on the captain's chair in front of the helm. Sure enough, the autopilot was on, heading us away from Catalina. I turned off the autopilot and brought the throttles back slowly to neutral, then picked up the handset of the marine radio and pressed the broadcast button.

"Coast Guard Sector LA, Coast Guard Sector LA, this is the power boat Flight Risk on Channel 16. I have an emergency, over." The radio crackled, and a disembodied voice answered softly then the signal got louder.

"Flight Risk this is Coast Guard Sector LA, what is the nature of your emergency, over?"

"I was abducted along with another woman who was being held against her will. We were being transported on Flight Risk by owner, Jonathan Chambers. He is now unconscious and secured. Requesting medical assistance. I've put the engines in neutral." I read out our current latitude and longitude.

"Flight Risk, this is Coast Guard Sector LA We have a vessel in the area and will intercept. Switch to Channel 22 Alpha for further comms, over."

"Roger, out."

I turned the buttons on the radio to 22A, a working channel used to free up 16 for other emergency calls.

After switching channels, I hailed them again. "Coast Guard Sector LA, this is Flight Risk on 22 Alpha, over." At the CG's request, I provided the number of persons on board, our conditions, and a description of the vessel. We were instructed to don life jackets and await their arrival. Rowan was standing beside me as I finished with the radio.

"What's happening with him?" I said, unable to get up to check in the cabin.

"He's still out but breathing. He's so tied up in rope they'll need a saw to get him free."

"Can you reach my phone in my jacket?" Rowan reached over and pulled out my phone, handing it to me. I put it down on the helm so I could work it with one hand. I pulled up my recent calls, clicked on Gordie's cell number, then handed her the phone. "Talk to him," I said. She had no idea who I meant. I had no energy left to explain.

Rowan was on the phone with Gordie in tears for a few minutes, then looked over at me.

"He's with someone named Barry and they're on their way to get us in Barry's boat. He wants to know our position." I read out our lat and long again into the phone.

"Tell him if they can get here before the Coast Guard, I'll buy them dinner." She continued talking into the phone, then put it down.

"He said to keep pressure on your shoulder and lock the cabin door in case Jonathan wakes up. He said to put out fenders on both sides of the boat. Not sure what that means, if it's not guitars."

There was a fat combination padlock hanging from the outside of the cabin door. Rowan grabbed it and put it through the metal clasps, locking the door. I gave Rowan directions on how to deploy the fenders that were sitting on top of the forward deck. She went up on deck, steadying herself with one hand on the rail and carefully tying two fenders each to the railings on the starboard and port sides. While she did that, I kept pressure on my shoulder, and rocked back and forth from the pain. I hoped to stay conscious. There was a lot of blood. My head pounded.

The chopper arrived first. The Coast Guard's orange flying machine hovered overhead, with a man in an orange suit and helmet hanging out the door having a look at us. Moments later, Barry's boat arrived.

Barry had absconded with someone's inflatable dingy from the marina and was towing it behind. Gordie jumped into it and started the outboard, gunning it over to Flight Risk. It wasn't difficult to board us since the seas had quieted down. I got up long enough to throw him a line and secure it to a cleat, then he pulled the dingy over to our starboard side and Rowan helped him tie it up so he could get on board. They hugged briefly. The noise from the helicopter, which had pulled further away but was still in earshot, precluded any conversation. Gordie came over to me and grabbed me as I started to go down, slipping off the seat.

CHAPTER THIRTY-SEVEN

In these lives that pass like minutes,
I'm not now trying to measure
the cosmic pieces
or the equanimity of time,
by the lines on my sword
or the things in my hand.

The Coast Guard's small boat rescue team arrived a few minutes after Barry and were joined by a Baywatch boat from Redondo, and a Sheriff's boat shortly thereafter. With the help of a Baywatch lifeguard, the Coasties got Rowan and me into the cabin of the Baywatch boat from Flight Risk for the ride to LA/Long Beach harbor. The Sheriff took charge of transporting the now conscious and handcuffed Jonathan, and Barry and Gordie headed back to Redondo on Barry's boat. I didn't know what happened to Flight Risk herself until later, when I was told that a Coastie drove her back to the impound dock at Terminal Island.

I didn't regain much control of my faculties until I found myself being transferred into an ambulance on dry land for a short ride, then wheeled into a hospital with an oxygen mask over my face.

The process of getting medically tended to and receiving a mere 4 or 5 stitches mostly escaped me. I did remember something about having a punctured pectoral muscle that missed all the vital structures and barely touched a lung. It was impressed upon me how lucky I was that the knife missed the neurovascular bundle right under my collar bone that contained nerves and large arteries, a puncture of which would have caused me to bleed to death.

I was kept overnight and given another x-ray in the morning to make sure my lung was OK, and a cat scan as well to make sure the bang on my head didn't cause permanent damage.

I could move my legs, arms, and put some thoughts together. That was all I cared about. The sling would come off in 48 hours, and the stitches out in 10 days.

After the fuss, I was dead tired and glad to be in a hospital bed and not having to talk to anyone. That didn't last long. Soon a parade of uniforms and those without uniforms but with IDs came through, asking me whether I was fit to answer some questions.

Mostly I said no, but I was unable to dodge the Special Agent.

"And you are?" I asked.

"McCall, from the LA Field Office," he said, as he put his ID away in his jacket pocket and pulled up a chair beside the bed. I hoped he wouldn't get too comfortable.

"What was going on with these Chambers guys, Agent McCall?"

"We'd had our eye on them for a while. The photos your team provided of Jonathan Chambers and Thorn disposing of a barrel in the sea were helpful."

I liked the sound of 'my team'. It made me feel important.

"What is the migrant connection?" I asked.

"Ongoing investigation. I can't tell you much, but I can say that there was an incident involving a waste disposal driver last month who was arrested with the body of a migrant in his vehicle."

"With a connection to Chambers, I assume. And he rolled over, as they do, to give you the smuggling connection."

"Ah, you might assume that."

"I will, thank you."

"I understand from your colleagues that you conducted extensive surveillance of Chambers. We'll need the full record of your investigation including all photographs. And we'll speak again when you're out of the hospital." He put a business card on the table beside me.

"Happy to help," I said.

Finally, Peter showed up to scold me for having gotten in such a mess.

"It made me fucking nervous, Mac. What were you thinking?"

"Is this about you, Peter?" He stuttered and I laughed, which kind of hurt various parts of my body.

"Sorry about that. I know you're pissed enough at me already. Rowan and Gordie and Barry, your three musketeers, are all out in the hallway trying to talk past the guards."

"What guards?"

"Well, nurses."

"Shit, I want a police guard. Or maybe Secret Service."

"I don't think you need it. The guy you and Rowan collared is under armed guard down the hall. Way down the hall."

"Good thing. He's going to sing like a canary, like they say in the movies. Kind of appropriate for the James Dean of waste management," I said.

CHAPTER THIRTY-EIGHT

Rowan and Gordie didn't get past the militant nurse who was holding the fort for the rest of the evening, but the doctors kept their promise to only keep me in overnight, which was fine with me since I hate hospitals. Gordie and Rowan met me in the hospital's circular driveway with his car when the nurse pushed me out in a wheelchair.

"Am I glad to see you," I said, slightly out of breath from the exertion of walking two steps from the wheelchair to the car's open backseat door. Before I shut the door, the nurse handed me a white paper bag that contained some pain pills and antibiotics.

"You okay there? Should I get the seat belt for you?" Gordie asked.

"I'll get in the back with her," Rowan said. She opened the front passenger door and came around to sit on the other side of me on the back seat.

"Sorry, still a bit woozy from something they gave me."

"I'll drive slowly," Gordie said. "No sudden turns. But if you need to puke, use that bag you were just handed."

"I'm good. They gave me an anti-nausea pill already." I looked over at Rowan. "I'd hug you if I wasn't strapped in and bandaged. How are you doing?"

"I'm okay. Got checked out at the hospital yesterday. It will take me awhile to get over the whole crazy thing."

"Right. I haven't spoken to your father yet, but I know you will have done."

"Gordie and I called him as soon as we got off the boat. We cried together. He said he wants to thank you in person. You should come back to Belfast with me."

"I'll gladly do that. What about you, Gordie? When is your current tour of photo duty over?"

"Soon. I'll just be a week behind you if you leave in the next few days. I'm taking you to my place now. I've a spare bedroom. Rowan is sleeping in my room and I'm on the couch." I didn't object. I was too exhausted.

"I want to hear the whole story, Rowan, or as much as you'd like to tell me."

"Soon, you get some rest first," she said.

"Where are we with the law enforcement people? Are there interviews to do or will they leave us alone for now?"

"Barry and I and Rowan already spoke to the cops and the feds. She gave her account of her abduction and captivity and identified Jonathan. They will want more, but I think for the moment at least, we're done."

"And Joe Thorn, too," Rowan added. "I didn't know who he was, but I was shown a photo by the FBI guy. Thorn was there when I was first brought to the house by Jonathan, and he came by every few days when Jonathan wasn't around. He delivered food and made sure I was locked up tight. Didn't say much."

"Were you tied up the whole time?" I didn't really want to hear the answer but felt like I had to ask.

"No, but I was in a locked room that just had a toilet, sink, a cot, chair, some books and an old tv. Jonathan said that if his brother or father thought I was still alive – if I was seen anywhere or word got out that I wasn't dead, that his family would have me killed."

"Christ," I said.

"And Jonathan said I wouldn't be locked up much longer. He was working on a way to get me out safely, so I could go back to Ireland. I pleaded to have him let me call my pa, but he was dead set against me contacting anyone."

"Of course he would have taken your phone away and pulled out the sim card if there was one."

"Yeah, he said it would get back to his family if I talked to anyone, and that it would be all over for me and him. He told his father and brother that I'd drowned in the harbor, that he'd made sure of it."

"Did he hurt you?"

"He didn't force himself on me at first, but that didn't last. He said he cared about me. Half the time he talked like a reasonable person, the other half he was unhinged and angry. It was..." Rowan caught herself starting to cry and wiped her eyes with her sleeve.

"He was a strange mixed-up guy, abducting you and disposing of bodies to the deep six for smugglers. Meanwhile he was trying in his own fucked up way to protect you," I said.

"I almost got out of there at one point, prying the board off one of the windows. When Thorn dropped off food he noticed. He secured it again with dozens of nails. My hands got pretty raw against the wood. I had nothing to use as tools. They only gave me plastic utensils." Rowan held out her hands to show red and scarred fingers."

"I'm so sorry Rowan," I said, not knowing what else to say.

"I washed clothes in the sink, did yoga, and tried not to think about what would happen every time he showed up."

I looked down at her feet. She was wearing red sneakers. "I heard about the red shoes."

"Time for a change of shoes," she said.

We arrived back at Gordie's apartment in Culver City, and after having a cup of tea and taking some of my prescription meds, I put on one of Gordie's t-shirts and went to sleep in his spare room. I asked Gordie to call Peter and Barry to let them know where I was and that I was still above ground. When I woke up, the sun was shining through the window, and I wondered for a moment where I was and how I'd gotten there.

"You'll want to go to your place and pick up some clothes, I expect?" Gordie asked me, when I walked into the kitchen, feeling disheveled and sore.

"Yes, please. I'm fine to drive. But I can't remember where I last left my car."

"I'll run you over there. Barry dropped your car off at your apartment this morning. It was in the marina parking lot at the Portofino."

"Where's Rowan?"

"She's out for a walk. Bloody happy to be out in the world again." Gordie rubbed the back of my neck gently while I sat at the kitchen table and stared at the wheat toast he'd made me.

"It'll take you awhile to get over this whole thing too, Mac."

"Except for this shoulder, I'm good. I won't be able to wash my hair until the stitches are out. I've got to go see my hair guy."

"Tomorrow's OK, right? No rush?"

"Yeah, tomorrow is fine. He doesn't do walk-ins anyway. He will have no sympathy. I have to make an appointment." Gordie laughed. It was good to see him smile. All was right in his world.

It took us several days to wrap up all of the communications with the FBI, who were taking the lead. Gordie and Barry were interviewed at length, sparing me some of the work, and the feds tread as light as they could on Rowan, which saved her from further trauma.

Rowan had meals with us but didn't talk much and spent a lot of time during the days staying in her room or going out to walk. Her only outing was going with her prior roommate, Jackie, to shop for some clothes. In the few evenings we were there, she was content to watch something on the screen while sitting beside Gordie, with her legs curled up on the couch, leaning against him. Neither Gordie nor I tried to get her to be more communicative, figuring that in time she would ease out of the shell she'd been forced into for the past month.

After several days recuperating at Gordie's, I made flight reservations from Los Angeles to Belfast via Dublin for Rowan and myself. I came off the heavy pain killers, got proficient at driving with just one hand, and arranged for my beloved Chris-Craft Speedster to get safely berthed up on a rack in the marina for the time being.

Peter showed up on the first day back in my own apartment. Unannounced as usual. He must have spies working for him to know when I'm home.

"Why are you here?" I asked, opening the door for him.

"Just thought I'd check on you."

I still felt too tired to deal with him, but there was a question that needed to be asked.

"How'd it go, meeting your long lost son?"

"He's good. Seems good. We got on."

"Where is he going to live and all that. Not that I really care."

Peter looked at me and shook his head. I wasn't sure what that meant.

"Maybe I could bring him over sometime soon. He's staying with his aunt for now, and I'll pay child support to her. I'm going to pick him up whenever I'm in town and do stuff with him."

"Maybe it will make you a more responsible adult," I said.

"Yeah, there's that possibility. What are your plans, Mac?" As we talked, still standing in the hallway, I was sorting the mail that had come to the apartment. There was a letter from the boat insurance carrier. I tore open the envelope and held out a document pertaining to my boat. It listed a dollar amount, but no check was issued yet. That would take longer, as expected with insurance companies.

"My insurance settlement, and by extension, my divorce settlement," I said.

"I'm so sorry about the boat. Will you get another? You were talking about a sailboat."

"I'm going to deposit the check when it comes. Meanwhile I'll put my few possessions back in storage, let go of this apartment, and take Rowan home. I don't know from there, but I think it's time I spent some time elsewhere."

CHAPTER THIRTY-NINE

We can't be measured.
We are defined by points of light
on a scale that reaches
to infinity,
beginning in the broad hills and mist
or along some waterfront,
as still as sound.

The flight from LA to Dublin was eleven hours. Daniel Collins bought us first class seats for the trip and was meeting us at the airport in Dublin for the couple hour drive to their home on the outskirts of Belfast, since there were no direct flights to the North from LAX. I had my own little cubby hole and a plane seat that became a bed, but still tossed around trying to find a comfortable position that didn't aggravate my shoulder. I finally dozed off for a couple of hours until it was lights on and breakfast being served.

Seeing the lush Irish coast come into view out the window filled me with emotion; a joy I hadn't felt in my body and head for some time.

When Rowan saw her father and brother waiting for us outside Customs, she dropped her bag and ran toward both as soon as she exited the door. I caught up with the group a few strides later. I still couldn't hug, having a left arm with limited mobility, but there were plenty of tears and hugs to go around.

After the initial greetings, I held back while they converged in a three-way hug and wept in unison. After a few minutes, Daniel disengaged and walked over to me. He was absolutely beaming. He gave me another light hug, conscious of my shoulder injury.

"I don't know how I can thank you enough, Mackenzie. You'll come back with us to the house, of course, and please be my guest for as long as you want," Daniel said.

"Actually, if you could please drop me in Cultra on the way, just a few blocks from the Culloden, that would be great. I've a delayed invitation to stay with my old friend there. But I will be in the neighborhood and would love to catch up with you all in the next few days."

"You'll just let me know, and we'll be there to fetch you for an afternoon or however long you'd like to stay with us. Please consider it your home," Daniel said.

Daniel dropped me off at Conan O'Donnell's house on the road to the Marino Station rail line, and Conan, who was expecting me, opened the door and ushered me and my suitcase into the warm and inviting foyer of his home.

"Come in Mackenzie, have a seat on the couch," he said, pointing me to the living room. He sat down in his big chair opposite me.

"So, you've got your lassie back home with her family in Belfast, and your bad man behind bars?"

"That man and all his waste disposal dynasty is now fully dismantled. They weren't murdering anybody, but they were occasionally disposing of the bodies of illegal migrants who didn't quite make it to America alive at the hands of some nasty people."

"And what was he planning to do with you and Rowan on that boat you were rescued from?"

"No telling, but it would not have been good. He was cornered and desperate."

"Well, it's all grand, Mackenzie. You didn't end up in the sea, and now you're here even if slightly wounded. How long can you stay?"

"A few days as your guest, if that's alright, while I get some walks in along the lough and get over my jet lag. And figure out where I'm going from here. I have some things to think about, including that my ex-husband just found out he has a son - as in he had a son while we were married, but he didn't find out until the mother passed away. Then he took his sweet time telling me."

"Well, that's a life changing event for him. How about for you?"

"It has nothing to do with me. But I might want to meet this little guy. He doesn't have a mom now. I'm continually mad at the ex, but maybe the kid would be fun."

"I know you never had children, but was that by choice?"

"We were postponing it for various logistical reasons with our jobs, then we broke up before we got there. One of several regrets."

Conan just smiled and left it at that. "Well let's get you a drink of something strong, and have you settled in the guest room."

Conan was a generous host, not minding over the next couple of days that I spent an inordinate amount of time sleeping between taking long walks and enjoying his fine company mostly for meals.

I begged off a visit to the newly reunited Collins family for the initial few days, wanting to give them time to heal and for Rowan to start the process of recovering from the emotional trauma of her abduction.

Belfast Lough is a long and wide sea inlet that stretches from the Irish Sea to the port of Belfast and the mouth of the River Lagan. The North Down Coastal Path along the lough has long been one of my favorite places to walk when visiting the North, with its large, lush expanses of parks, walkways along its windy coast, and breathtaking sunsets over the water.

Watching the red sky fading at last light over the lough on my third evening, I made the decision to keep to the European and British sides of the world, at least for a time. With my close family gone, my ex-partner off onto his next chapter, my floating home destroyed, and the current investigation concluded, there wasn't much drawing me back to California's parched ground. I kicked at the sand and scree as I walked along the shore of the lough. I could find some healing myself on this green isle.

Made in the USA
Las Vegas, NV
01 February 2024

85161381R00163